NGOLO DIASPORA

BALOGUN OJETADE
MILTON DAVIS

MVmedia, LLC
Fayetteville, GA

MVmedia, LLC
PO Box 143052
Fayetteville, GA 30214
www.mvmediaatl.com

Publisher's Note: This is a work of fiction. Names, characters, places, and incidents are a product of the author's imagination. Locales and public names are sometimes used for atmospheric purposes. Any resemblance to actual people, living or dead, or to businesses, companies, events, institutions, or locales is completely coincidental.

Book Layout ©2017BookDesignTemplates.com

Ordering Information:
Quantity sales. Special discounts are available on quantity purchases by corporations, associations, and others. For details, contact the "Special Sales Department" at the address above.

Ngolo/ Balogun Ojetade/Milton Davis. -- 1st ed.
ISBN 978-1-7346279-6-1

Contents

We dedicate this novella to Chadwick Boseman, who helped bring about the latest wave of love for Black Speculative Fiction.

CHAPTER ONE

The Near Future...

The night air was still. But on the grounds outside of Stanton Mansion, it was anything but.

Secret Service agents patrolled the grounds of the mansion of Majority Leader of the New Republic Party, Senator Patrick Stanton. The men and women that patrolled on foot close to the house wore navy blue trousers, white shirts, navy blue ties and gray blazers. The agents that patrolled further out on four-wheeled ATVs were clad in charcoal gray jumpsuits and combat boots. All of them were armed with pistols and each agent on foot also carried a short-barreled shotgun slung across his or her shoulder while the agents on vehicular patrol were armed with HK-MP5 assault rifles.

They walked with confidence. Who would dare come onto the Stanton Estate uninvited? And if they did, they would quickly go back where they came from... or to Hell.

A man in a well-tailored, black shark-skin suit walked around the back of the mansion, checking the doors and windows. The man spoke and a red light flashed on his earpiece—" This is Chief Colby. How's it looking out there?"

A man's voice came through Colby's earpiece, "This is Red Team Leader. All is safe and secure on the outer perimeter."

"This is Blue Team Leader," a woman's voice followed. "We're looking good on the inner perimeter, sir.

"Outstanding," Colby said. "All's well on the interior. The package is wrapped tight for the night. All's quiet. Let's keep it that way."

But a figure concealed in shadow, just outside the mansion's perimeter, watched... and waited.

* * *

Inside the sprawling mansion, Senator Patrick Stanton and his wife, Diana, slept peacefully in their king-size rice bed, only their heads and necks poking out from under white, 1000-thread-count Egyptian cotton bed sheets.

On the floor below, their butler, Jeremy, sat in the library reading the classic novel, Meji: Book 2, while sipping bourbon from a Denver and Liely bourbon glass. He peered through the space between the thick brown velvet curtains at the Secret Service Agents walking past a row of bushes near the fountain several yards away then he returned to his book, just missing a bush stir, then rise, revealing a tall man in a ghillie suit.

The man quickly removed the ghillie suit, revealing a black, skin-tight jumpsuit underneath. His thin brown fingers reached into the ghillie suit and snatched out a black utility vest hidden within. With lightning speed, he slipped on the vest as he sprinted toward the mansion. He pulled out a sheet of yellow paper from a pocket on the vest and unfolded it as he ran.

A Secret Service Agent sauntered around the corner of the mansion, softly humming a tune. His eyes widened and his jaw went slack when he spotted the man just a few yards away.

"The Mailman," the agent gasped.

The Mailman tossed the sheet of paper in the air then hurled a throwing knife through the top of it. The knife slammed into the agent's chest, nailing the sheet of paper to his torso. The Mailman then kicked the pommel of the knife, sinking the knife deeper into the agent's body and sending him flying into the front door of the mansion. The crash echoed through the mansion foyer and up the stairs.

Startled awake, Senator Stanton and his wife sat bolt upright in bed.

"What the hell," Stanton whispered, staring at his wife.

He leapt out of bed and grabbed an old Louisville slugger baseball bat that leant against his nightstand. Diana reached under her pillow and slipped on the brass knuckles hidden there. The Stantons marched out of their room and charged toward the stairway. Jeremy met them there.

"Jeremy, what the hell is going on?" Stanton asked. "Where's Chief Colby?"

"It appears there's been a security breach, sir," Jeremy said, his posh British accent thick. "I don't think it's wise for you and Mrs. Stanton to be out and about right now."

"This is my house, Jer'," Stanton said. "I'm not letting some burglar make me tremble and I'm not hiding in my bedroom!"

"It was not a burglar, Senator Stanton," Jeremy said. "It appears someone is trying to enter through the front door, sir."

"Follow me!" Senator Stanton ordered, scurrying down the stairs.

Diana followed her husband, holding her fist close to her chin like a boxer. Jeremy rolled his eyes and bounded down the stairs behind her, much more athletic than his gray hair would indicate.

Senator Stanton, Diana and Jeremy crept toward the door. The Senator took up a position on the side of the door. Diana stood behind him. Jeremy stood in front of the door, his knees bent deeply and hands out in front of him like a collegiate wrestler. Stanton raised the bat above his head.

"Open it," the Senator whispered.

Jeremy looked at Stanton, his face a mask of fear. He shook his head.

Senator Stanton rolled his eyes. "Damn it, Jeremy, open the door," he ordered.

Jeremy swallowed hard and then snatched the door open. He jumped back in fear as Stanton prepared to swing the bat.

The dead Secret Service Agent fell into the doorway and collapsed onto the granite floor.

Jeremy screamed like a teenage girl victim in a horror movie.

"My God!" Diana gasped, looking down at the agent's corpse in horror.

"Damn it!" the Senator spat.

Chief Colby rushed into the room from behind the Senator. Senator Stanton snapped his head toward him.

"It took you long enough, Chief!" Stanton spat.

"My apologies, sir, but our communications were temporarily down," Chief Colby said. "At last check, all was quiet."

"But I spoke with you. You told me that there was a security breach," Jeremy said.

Chief Colby shook his head. "Wasn't me," Colby said. "We only came running because we heard your wife scream, Senator."

Stanton and Diana exchanged glances. Jeremy swallowed hard and tried to divert the conversation.

"Umm...Chief, what is that on the agent's chest?" Jeremy asked, pointing at the corpse's torso. "It appears to be held in place by that dagger."

"Very observant, Jeremy," Colby said with a smirk. "The One World Union is safe because of your untiring efforts and eagle eye."

Chief Colby bent down and inspected

the Agent's dead body. He removed the sheet and perused the writing on it. He looked up from the body, his expression one of deep concern. Colby handed the sheet to Jeremy. Stanton looked from Colby to Jeremy.

"What?" the Senator asked.

Jeremy's eyes widened as he read the sheet of paper.

The senator released a heavy sigh. "For God's sake, read it aloud, man!" he shouted.

"It says 'Minority Leader of the Real Party, Senator Harvey McCarthy, has issued this contract on the life of Senator Patrick Stanton, in accordance with International Law, set forth at the Beijing Conference of A.D. 2063'," Jeremy replied.

"What?" Senator Stanton said, shocked.

"That son-of-a-bitch!" Stanton spat. He smashed a vase with the baseball bat, sending pieces of porcelain flying about the room. "That goddamned son-of-a-bitch! He put a fucking hit out on me?"

"It gets worse, sir," Jeremy said. "The contract was served by the Bloodmen!"

Stanton's face went pale. His left eye jumped and his top lip quivered.

"Bloo-Bloodmen?" Stanton stuttered. "Impossible! That bastard couldn't afford to hire the Bloodmen. Not without party backing. Then the person who did this was the—"

"The Mailman," Chief Colby chimed in.

"Oh, God," Diana croaked.

Senator Stanton snapped his head toward his head of security. "What the hell are you just standing around for, Colby? Get the hell out of here and search the grounds!"

* * *

The Mailman calmly walked away from the Stanton Estate as Secret Service Agents frantically searched the property. He slipped in his ear bud and spoke, "The contract has been successfully delivered. One casualty."

"Excellent," a voice said in his ear. "Come on in for debriefing."

"I'm on my way," the Mailman said.

He sprinted off, disappearing into shadow.

CHAPTER TWO

Among all the swanky hotels in the world, the *Wyndsor*, on Chicago's Magnificent Mile, was considered one of the very best, combining Hong Kong's cosmopolitan flair with the Windy City's urban charm. A chocolate sommelier created custom sweets for guests, and even pets were pampered with an in-room dining menu and doggie massages.

The staff looked like they had been snatched off the cover of Vogue magazine; even the custodians and housekeepers. One of those beautiful housekeepers rushed into the employee's lounge, her braids dancing on the black collar of her maroon shirt with each step. Her hard muscles moved under her shirt and black cotton trousers as she sat down at a desk to sign in on the laptop.

A lean man, immaculately dressed in a burgundy sharkskin two-piece suit, glided over to her, wagging his finger.

"Christina, you're late again," he said.

The woman shrugged. "At least I'm here," she said, her Brazilian accent thick.

"Don't get smart with me, Ms. Thang!"

the man hissed. "I'll have your ass back on a flight to Bahia before you can yell Carnaval!" He snapped his fingers.

The woman gave the man a hard-stare. He swallowed nervously. A smile spreads across the woman's face and she kissed him on the cheek.

"Silly man," the young woman chuckled. "That's what I love about you, Victor... always joking... right?"

She locked eyes with Victor again. Her eyes were cold, even though she still wore a smile.

Victor took a step back.

Christina giggled and then skipped off.

* * *

Christina rode the elevator with only her cart of cleaning supplies to keep her company. She got off on the twelfth floor and pushed her cart to room 1215 then rapped on the door with her fist.

A pudgy Caucasian man, with white hair in a mess all over his head, opened the door a bit and peeked out.

"Yes?" he inquired.

"Housekeeping," Christina crooned.

"No need, gorgeous," the man said. "I'm fine."

Christina winked at the man and gave him a sly smile. "You sure are."

Not half as fine as you, chocolate drop," the man said. "I guess my room could use a bit of tidying up after all."

The man opened the door and Christina sauntered into the room, smiling seductively at him and pushing her cart inside with her round bottom.

"So, what's your name, baby?"

"Christina Santana."

"Brazilian or Cuban?" the man asked.

"Brazilian," she said.

The man slowly ran his tongue across his thin lips. "Sexy," he said. "My name's Trent. Trent Baker. Pleasure to meet you, Christina."

"I'm sure it will be a pleasure when you... *meat* me, hun," Christina said, looking him up and down.

"You're something else," Trent said, blushing.

"Come here," she said, beckoning him with a wave of her index finger. "Let me show you exactly what I am."

Trent sauntered over to Christina, who pushed his shoulders, spinning Trent around until his back was to her. She began rubbing her hands up his butt.

Trent chuckled. "Ooh, kinky!"

Christina slowly worked her fingers up his back as she breathed into Trent's ear. He moaned in ecstasy.

Christina reached Trent's neck. She caressed it for a moment and then, suddenly wrapped her forearms around his neck, locking on a tight rear-naked choke. She squeezed, choking Trent into unconsciousness then let him fall on the bed.

"Sorry, lover," Christina said. Her Brazilian accent was now replaced by a Southern American one. "I need your view."

Christina reached under the cart and withdrew the parts to a sniper rifle. She quickly and adeptly assembled it and then stepped out onto the balcony. She looked through the scope down at the pool. There were several people swimming and more sitting by the pool. Jamela spotted her target, a middle-aged man with skin nearly as red as his hair. He was surrounded by five bodyguards.

Christina smiled. "Hi Dr. Billups," she said cheerily. "Hi bodyguards."

She slipped a small, white silicone bud into her ear.

"This is Jamela Rashon, confirming contract," she said softly.

A woman's rich alto voice came from her ear bud, "The target has not complied with the wishes of our client," it said. "The contract is valid. Proceed!"

Jamela fired.

A moment later, Dr. Billups' skull exploded and his limp body fell into the pool. People screamed and ran away from the pool. Jamela calmly broke down the rifle and put it back under her cart. She looked at Trent. He was beginning to stir.

"Thanks for a great time, Romeo," she said, pushing the cart toward the door.

Jamela left Trent's room then walked briskly toward the elevator.

Reaching the elevator, she pressed the button to go down.

After a short while, the elevator door opened. Victor stood on the elevator with four men in cheap suits. Jamela could tell from experience that they were police detectives.

Two of them grabbed Jamela's arms as a third searched her cart. He pulled out the case and opened it, showing it to the fourth detective.

"Barrett M82, sir," the third detective said to the fourth.

Victor stepped off the elevator, jabbing his finger toward Jamela. "That's her," he shouted. "Christina Santana. I knew she wasn't right. I knew it!"

"Ms. Santana, is it?" the fourth detective asked, stepping toward her.

"It's Jamela Rashon, actually." Jamela replied.

The fourth detective glanced at Victor then looked back at Jamela.

"Well, Ms. Rashon, I'm Detective Sergeant John Roberts," the fourth detective said. "I must, by law, inform you that you are under arrest for murder."

"Damn, you got here quick!" Jamela said, looking at the detective impressed.

"We eat lunch here at this time every Tuesday," Detective Sergeant Roberts said.

"Just my luck," Jamela said. "Well, Sergeant, I can explain. I'm a Bloodman. The man I just neutralized was the subject of a legitimate contract."

"A Bloodman, eh?" Detective Sergeant Roberts said. "Let me see your authorization."

Jamela reached into her blouse and retrieved her documents. She tossed them to the Detective Sergeant. He looked over the papers and glanced up at Jamela, who was smiling.

"Your paperwork's in order, but your method of assassination doesn't coincide with the methods of the Guilds," Detective Sergeant Roberts said. "So, I'm gonna have to contact your Guildmaster for verification. If he corroborates your story, you're free to go."

Detective Sergeant Roberts pulled up his sleeve, revealing a rectangular video screen and keyboard that lit up under his skin. He began typing in numbers on the keyboard.

* * *

Two men sat in leather high-backed chairs, watching a huge television screen that nearly took up the entire length of wall in the conference room.

The older man was tall and handsome, with smooth, dark skin accented by a well-trimmed mustache and goatee and short, black hair. Although he was in his fifties, he stood tall and regal with the physique of a bodybuilder.

The other man was in his thirties, of a medium-brown complexion, with a head full of brown locks. He was as muscular as the older man, but even bigger and taller, but not quite as majestic. Although he was taller than the other man, he lacked his poise.

On the television screen, a woman dressed in a blue pencil skirt and white blouse stood in front of the mansion of Senator Patrick Stanton.

"In political news, Channel Two has learned that Senator Harvey McCarthy has served Senator Patrick Stanton a contract of assassination," she began. "Although both parties refuse to comment on the situation, sources say that the contract stems from Senator Stanton's refusal to negotiate on the Anti-Assassination Bill due for voting in two weeks."

The camera drew closer to the woman reporting the news.

"What is even more astonishing is that Senator McCarthy has retained the services of the Bloodmen Guild," she went on. "Some are questioning how McCarthy could have raised the funds necessary to hire such an expensive guild; a guild that is said to be the oldest and most efficient."

The younger man turned off the television.

"This isn't good, Master Kamara," the young man said.

"We are doing our job, Stephen," Master Kamara said. "That's all."

"You know what I'm talking about," Stephen said, frowning. "Accepting the contract on Senator Stanton was purely political. Everyone knows Senator McCarthy can't afford us and the party would not provide the funds."

"They will speculate, but they won't ask outright," Kamara said. "Stanton will meet with McCarthy and vote to maintain the Guilds."

"This is dangerous, Kamara," Stephen said. "You are jeopardizing this Guild by getting involved in this dispute."

"In case you haven't noticed, Stephen, this Guild is already in jeopardy."

Stephen slammed his fist into his palm. "Don't play me for a fool, Kamara! Pro bono contracts aren't allowed, according to the Beijing Convention and McCarthy didn't pay!"

"Don't quote protocol to me, son," Kamara said. "I am your Master."

"That you are," Stephen said with a nod. "But I'm a third-generation Bloodman. My grandfather was at the Conference. He founded the Bloodmen and my father—"

"Your father stepped down and made me Master of this Ile because I am from a line of African martial masters that stretches back to the days when the pyramids were still young," Kamara said, interrupting him. "My knowledge far exceeds any Bloodman to ever sit in this most sacred of places and still, I carry myself as everyone's brother... and friend."

Stephen scowled at Kamara. "I wonder what the other Guilds would say about your actions."

Kamara snapped his head toward Stephen. "What are *you* saying?"

The television screen blinked on. Detective Sergeant Roberts' face appeared on-screen.

"Master Keita?" The detective asked.

Kamara nodded. "Yes. How may I help you?"

"I'm police detective Sergeant John Roberts," he said. "I apologize for the interruption, but we have a situation here that we need you to help us with."

"Go on, Sergeant," Kamara said.

"Thank you," Roberts said. "We have a woman here claiming to be one of yours. She assassinated a Dr. Peter Billups less than twenty minutes ago. Her papers check out, but we're skeptical. She used a Barretta M82 sniper rifle to kill Dr. Billups. I thought it is forbidden for Guilds to use firearms to fulfill contracts."

"It is not our preferred method, but it is not a taboo," Kamara said. "It is a compliment to your exemplary protection of your city that she had to resort to such methods. I presume the woman you refer to is Ms. Jamela Rashon?"

"Yes sir."

"She is indeed one of ours, Sergeant."

"Thank you. She is free to go, then," Detective Sergeant Roberts said. "She would like to speak to you before we sign off, though."

"Thank you, Detective Sergeant Roberts," Kamara said.

Jamela appeared on the screen, smiling.

Kamara greeted her with a warm smile.

Stephen rolled his eyes.

"Master, it's good to see you!" Jamela said.

"I see you are staying out of trouble, as always," Kamara said.

"Just doing my job, Papa," Jamela said.

"In the future, try to do it according to tradition."

"If you say so, Papa."

"I do," Kamara said. "Will you be returning home for Founders' Day?"

"Forgive me, Papa, but you know how I feel about such things," Jamela said. She lowered her gaze. "I'm not exactly a legacy."

"Nor am I, child," Kamara said. "But I am respectful of our heritage. You should try being the same."

"Will Malcolm be there?" Jamela asked.

"Yes, my son will be there," Kamara replied. "He should be returning from Japan soon."

Jamela smiled. "Then, I'll see you on Founders' Day!"

"Don't just come for Malcolm," Kamara said. "Come to see your future father-in-law! It's been a while."

"You're making me blush, Papa!" Jamela chuckled. "I'll be there to see you and Malcolm."

The screen went black. Kamara turned to Stephen to see his ever-present frown.

"I don't approve of her ways," Stephen said, turning up his nose.

"She is a bit...rough," Kamara said. "But she's one of our best."

"Will Malcolm really be here?" Stephen asked.

"Of course, he will; as soon as he is done in Nagano."

CHAPTER THREE

Nagano, Japan

Snow cascaded from the gray clouds, blanketing the tiled roof of the shiru that loomed in the distance and covering the grounds in white.

An army of men and women, clad in yoroi—the all black, hooded garb commonly worn by ninja—swarmed about. They were members of the Ronin Guild, and they had been hired to protect Toshi Tanaka, owner of *Nakite Shipping*. The Guildmaster of the Ronin, Ai Sasaki, stood among the assassins, wearing a black and gold kimono with a matching obi belt and black split-toe socks and wooden sandals. A short sword in a black scabbard protruded from her obi. She shouted orders.

"Move quickly," she said. "He is here somewhere."

A man wearing a uniform similar to the rank-and-file ninja—except the edge of his jacket, as well as his arm and leg wraps, were red—ran past Ai.

Ai grabbed the man's arm, spinning him around until they faced each other.

"Hideshi! Is Tanaka secure?" she asked.

"Yes, Guildmaster Ai," Hideshi replied. "His double is departing in the limo, as planned. Mr. Tanaka is in the guest quarters."

"Good!" Ai said. "Keep the attention focused on the limo, Guild Professor. That should distract our adversary."

Hideshi whirled about and ran off.

Ai briskly walked to the guesthouse. Ronin Assassins surrounded the building, hidden in shadow. She looked around to ensure it was safe to go in and then she unlocked the door.

Someone rammed their body into Ai, knocking her through the door and into the guesthouse, startling Tanaka. The diminutive executive was in his late sixties, with balding white hair and liver-spotted skin. Tanaka sat on a sleeper sofa in the sparsely furnished open space of the guest house flanked by ronin.

Ai fell to her knees.

Standing in the doorway behind her was an athletically built Black man holding a pair of ada short swords at his side. The man looked like a younger version of the Bloodmen's Guildmaster, Kamara Keita. He wore indigo tactical pants and tactical shirt with a royal blue Ankara pattern, and black tactical boots.

Tanaka and three Ronin leapt to their feet as Ai struggled to stand.

"Ai! What is going on?" Tanaka shouted.

"It's Malcolm Keita!" she shouted. "Stop him!"

The first Ronin leapt toward Malcolm, his sword held high, while simultaneously, the second Ronin crept toward him in a low crouch, sword drawn and the third charged at him.

The first Ronin descended. Malcolm slashed upward. He then held his ada out to the side, shoulder height. Blood dripped from the tip of the blade and splashed on the wooden floor. The Ronin fell at Malcolm's feet, his face a mask of agony. His leg, from the knee down, lay a few feet away from him.

Malcolm evaded the creeping Ronin's low slash at his legs as he chopped one ada down into Ronin's shoulder and thrust the other short sword into the third Ronin's gut.

Lightning fast, Malcolm then withdrew the ada that was in the third Ronin's gut and used it to decapitate the second Ronin. The ninja's hooded head rolled across the floor.

He then used the sword that was embedded in the decapitated Ronin's shoulder to hack into the side of the third Ronin's neck.

The Ronin fell, blood spurting from his neck with each beat of his failing heart.

Malcolm walked over the bodies of the three downed Ronin toward Tanaka, who held his hands before him, terrified.

"No! No!" Tanaka yelled in a panic.

Tanaka turned to run. Malcolm exploded forward, his hand moving in a quick, downward arc.

Ai suddenly leapt between Tanaka and Malcolm, her sword drawn and at the ready.

Hideshi charged into the guest house with his sword drawn.

"Get Tanaka out of here, now," Ai ordered Hideshi "I'll deal with this Bloodman."

Hideshi lowers his sword. "Mistress Ai—
"

Ai does not take her eyes off of Malcolm.

"It is too late," Hideshi croaks.

Ai looks confused. "What?"

She looks over her shoulder. Her eyes widen.

Tanaka lies face down on the floor, a dagger protruding from the back of his skull.

Ai snapped her head back to Malcolm, her face twisted into a mask of anger and pain. She unleashed a blood-chilling scream as she skittered forward, attacking Malcolm with blinding speed.

Malcolm calmly parried and evaded Ai's sword, never striking back.

Hideshi thrusted his sword between Ai and Malcolm, blocking Ai's slash.

"Shihan, no!" Tanaka said. "You are risking Vendetta!"

More Ronin rushed into the guesthouse. Upon seeing Tanaka's dead body, they rushed to help Hideshi stop Ai, grabbing her arms. Ai kicked a Ronin away from her. The other Ronin yanked Ai's arms behind her back, subduing her. Hideshi pulled her sword from Ai's trembling fingers.

"A curse on you, Bloodman!" Ai hissed.

"You bring shame upon your Guild, Mistress Ai," Malcolm said, pointing an ada at her. "This is a closed contract, executed according to all our laws and customs. You had no right to attack me."

"To hell with the law," Ai shouted. "You have murdered my father!"

Malcolm shook his head. "You accepted a protection contract from your own father?"

Ai fell to her knees in tears.

Hideshi approached Malcolm.

"I tried to talk her out of it," he said. "But she insisted. She knew this contract belonged to the Bloodmen, but she could not convince her father to meet with the union that hired you."

"I didn't know," Malcolm said.

"Would it have changed your mind if you did?" Hideshi asked.

"No."

Hideshi bowed to Malcolm.

"You must leave now," Hideshi said. "Mistress Ai will wish to take her own life. I must assist her."

Malcolm returned Hideshi's bow by lowering his gaze and tapping his swords together in an 'X'.

"Congratulations on your promotion to Guildmaster, then," Malcolm said. "I am sure you will serve your Guild well."

Malcolm backed out the door and turned to leave.

"It is a cruel profession we have chosen," Hideshi said.

Malcolm looked over his shoulder at Hideshi. "Cruel, indeed."

Malcolm walked away, leaving the new Guildmaster to help the former die.

CHAPTER FOUR

Black men and women of all ages trained together in the capacious room—some sparred with wooden swords; others grappled, deftly throwing each other on the sand-colored puzzle mats that covered the floor; and others played Capoeira Angola, trying to outwit and outmaneuver each other in a chess-like game of kicks, foot-sweeps, headbutts, knee strikes and elbows. They all wore blood red dashiki with no pattern and matching trousers.

The Goma and Teke masks that line the blue walls seemed to watch in judgment.

Guildmaster Kamara, dressed in a white dashiki with long sleeves and white trousers, stood observing his brothers and sisters. He shook his head, disappointed at what he saw.

"Ago!" he shouted, ordering them to pay attention.

"Ame!" the Bloodmen shouted in response, confirming that they were paying attention.

Kamara paced back and forth before the Bloodmen. "To wrestle, by African standards, is to put your opponent where?" he asked the crowd.

"On his back, belly, or side, sir!" The Bloodmen answered in unison.

"In order to make him more vulnerable to what?" Kamara asked.

"A finishing technique, sir!" the Blood-men replied.

"A what?"

"A finishing technique, sir!" the Blood-men shouted even louder.

"Then put your opponent down," Kamara said. "The method is unimportant—foot-sweep; knockout with an elbow; killing him with an arrow through the chest—it doesn't matter, but he or she must fall!"

Kamara stopped pacing and stood before the Bloodmen, his expression hard as stone.

"This is the goal of every Bloodman in combat," he went on. "Yebo?"

"Yebo, Oluwo Kamara!" they shouted in agreement with their master. "Yebo!"

The Bloodmen resumed training, with a fervor and ferocity that would have sent lesser partners to their grave.

Stephen sauntered into the hall dressed in the Bloodmen's training uniform. His uniform was red like the rank-and-file Bloodmen, but his dashiki had long sleeves. He knelt before Kamara in the traditional salute, with his left hand raised in front of his forehead, palm outward and his right fist touching the floor next to his right knee.

Kamara returned the salute then stood. Stephen followed suit.

"A rare visit, Stephen," Kamara said with a slight smile. "What brings you here?"

"As much as this pains me, Oluwo, I cannot stand by and watch you take the Guild down this path," Stephen replied.

The Bloodmen stopped training to witness the conflict between the Guild Professor and their Guildmaster.

"What path are you referring to?" Kamara inquired.

"You know exactly what I'm talking about," Stephen said, thrusting an index finger toward the Guildmaster. "Tell the Brotherhood why you have broken tradition and have agreed to run on the ticket with Senator Harvey McCarthy as the Vice President of the United States."

The Bloodmen looked shocked. Kamara remained calm.

"Where did you get this information?" Kamara asked.

"So, you don't deny it?" Stephen said.

"No. I was going to announce it at Founders' Day, in fact," Kamara said. "I ask again, though... how did you come by this information, Stephen?"

"That doesn't matter," Stephen spat. "We can't align ourselves with a political party. This goes against everything we stand for!"

"These are different times, Stephen," Kamara said. He placed a gentle hand on Stephen's thick shoulder. "Do you think Patrick Stanton is the only politician who wants to see an end to the Assassin Guilds?"

Stephen shrugged Kamara's hand off of him.

Briefly, an expression of sadness came across Kamara's face then his look of serenity returned.

"Around the globe, people are denouncing our profession as barbaric and unnecessary," he went on. "People that are more powerful than you can imagine. The Guilds must evolve to survive."

"The Guilds must be what they are," Stephen said. "Nothing more and nothing less. We grease the wheels of power; we make sure that important decisions are not lost in endless arguments and stalemates. This is our only function."

"What better place to do that than from within?" Kamara said with a slight smile.

"Enough of this!" Stephen shouted.

He turned to the ranks of Bloodmen. "I want you all to hear what I have to say," he began. "You are my witnesses."

He turned back toward Kamara and said loudly, "Kamara Keita, I challenge you for leadership of the Bloodmen Guild of Assassins."

Kamara frowned. "You cannot be serious."

"As cancer," Stephen said, glaring at Kamara. "Meet me in the Circle for Ijala Combat, or step down immediately!"

"This won't be playing Capoeira in the roda, Stephen. This will be Ijakadi—the way we do it back home. Blood will be shed."

"You presume because I wasn't born in Mother Africa, I'm ignorant of the old ways," Stephen said. "I know exactly what Ijala Combat entails. And only *your* blood will feed the Circle today!"

Kamara keeps his gaze on Stephen as he calls out, "Akingbe!"

A very tall Bloodman snaps to attention. "Yes, Oluwo," Akingbe shouts.

"Notify the senior Bloodmen," Kamara says. "Tell them that a challenge has been declared in front of witnesses. Tell them to prepare for Ijala."

"Yebo!" Akingbe shouts. He then sprints out of the training hall.

"I tried to be patient, Oluwo," Stephen said to Kamara. "I knew you were getting older and I was willing to wait for my opportunity to lead, but you began this political nonsense. I won't allow you to destroy this Ile before I have had my chance to be Oluwo and to lead this Guild the right way... the traditional way."

"Ipa abere lokun nto," Kamara said in Yoruba.

"It is the path blazed by the needle that the thread follows," Stephen translated. He rolled his eyes and pushed air forcefully from his nostrils. "Humph!"

Stephen turned and sauntered away.

Kamara watched him leave, clenching his fists tightly at his sides.

CHAPTER FIVE

The Bloodmen stood around the Warriors' Circle, a fighting ring composed of sand, ringed by stones. A band of drummers entered the Circle, playing a war-song on their shekere, djembe, dundun and talking drums.

The Bloodmen were pumped up and eager to see the battle. They clapped as Stephen entered the Circle dressed in black shorts, and black hand-wraps.

Stephen did a war-dance around the Circle and then stood strong in the center.

Kamara approached the Circle and the Bloodmen roared, cheering and applauding.

The drummers played furiously.

Kamara, wearing red shorts and red hand-wraps, did his war-dance around Stephen and then faced him in the center of the Circle.

The men saluted each other, stood and then backed up to their respective edges of the ring of sand. The drum beat quickened.

Stephen leapt forward.

Kamara charged to meet him.

The fight had begun.

Stephen landed on all fours and with his hands on the ground, whipped a spinning back-heel-kick at Kamara's head.

Kamara bent backward allowing the kick to sail just over his face.

He then countered with a powerful cross-punch.

Stephen put his wrists together, forming an 'X' with his forearms, then deflected the crushing blow with a "Skull and Bones" block with the tip of his elbow.

Stephen followed with a hook-punch that Kamara blocked with the side of his elbow, held high at the side of his head.

Stephen leapt forward with a knee toward Kamara's liver.

Kamara dropped his stance and slammed the point of his elbow downward into the front of Stephen's thigh.

Stephen grimaced in agony as pain radiated up his thigh. He staggered as his leg went limp.

Kamara took advantage of Stephen's disorientation wrought by pain and wrapped his arms around Stephen's waist.

The Guildmaster yanked Stephen into the air then slammed him to the ground *hard*.

A cloud of sand rose from where Stephen was thrown.

The drummers drummed faster, harder and the Bloodmen cheered.

Stephen lay in a twisted heap. Kamara stood over him with his hand outstretched.

"A ki i da owo le ohun ti a o le gbe," Kamara said. "Do not lay hands on a load you cannot lift."

Stephen looked up angrily. "Get away from me," he spat.

Kamara kept his hand outstretched. "It's over. Let me help you."

"I said, get away from me," Stephen cried. "I won't let you destroy the Bloodmen!"

Stephen struggled to his feet, gasping for breath. Bloodmen tried to help him, but he shoved them away.

"Ijala is over," Kamara said. "Accept the outcome."

"I am no longer a Bloodman," Stephen said. "I don't answer to you anymore."

Stephen stomped off, leaving everyone staring at him in stunned silence.

"You can't just quit the Bloodmen," Kamara shouted at Stephen's back. "You know what the consequences of that are."

Stephen stopped and turned to face Kamara. He stormed back toward him. Kamara remained calm.

"I know exactly what the consequences are," Stephen said. "Who's going to do it? You?"

Stephen looked into the crowd of Bloodmen.

"Which one of you, huh?" Stephen glared at the Bloodmen that stood before him. "Which one of you is going to kill me?"

Stephen angrily spat blood onto the ground. No one said anything. No one moved.

"I thought so," Stephen said. He turned his attention back to the Guildmaster. "See, this is what happens when you ignore tradition, Kamara. I commit the worst crime a Bloodman can commit and no one has the nerve to mete out punishment. We kill strangers for a living, but we can't punish our own. Pathetic! I will stop you, Kamara. I promise you, I will!"

Stephen stormed out of the hall.

Kweku, one of the senior Bloodmen, drew his knife and moved to go after him.

Kamara grabbed Kweku's wrist, stopping him.

"No, Kweku; let him go," Kamara said. "Stephen will return once he's cooled down. I know he will."

CHAPTER SIX

In the foyer of Bones' Steakhouse, gilded padding wrapped around stairway rails and an antique bust sat near an ornate chair that could double, in a pinch, as a throne. Painted portraits of royalty from different nations and dynasties hung on a craggy white brick wall, doused in eerie light from wrought-iron fixtures across the room that reflected the glow of the crystal chandeliers overhead.

Stephen sauntered in, dressed in a denim jacket over a white dress shirt, blue jeans and brown Chelsea boots—a far cry from his Bloodmen's uniform.

"Hello, sir. Welcome to Bones'," the Maître D' said with a broad smile.

"I have a reservation," Stephen said dryly.

"Your name, sir?" the Maître D' asked.

"Stephen Jones."

The Maître D' checked the list. He nodded. "Follow me, sir."

The Maître D' led Stephen into the posh dining area to a hand-carved mahogany table set for eight. Stephen sat down in one of the red leather chairs and waited. A few moments later, a man he recognizes enters the restaurant and approaches Stephen's table.

The man was tall and thin, his skin a smooth, light yellow-brown. His raven hair was brushed back into a ponytail that lay on the back of his burnt orange blazer.

The man sauntered over to Stephen's table, his perfect smile growing broader the closer he approached.

"Gilberto," Stephen said, standing to shake the man's hand. "On time, as usual." He looked at his watch. "Where are the others?"

"They aren't coming," Gilberto said. "I'm here as a representative."

Stephen frowned. "What do you mean, they aren't coming? I sent out a Level Six Guild request."

"Yes, you did, but you are not Guildmaster; Kamara is," Gilberto said, turning up his nose. "The other Guildmasters and Guild Professors went to your... how do you say... 'ee-lay'?"

"Yes, Ile," Stephen said softly. "So, they know."

"Yes, they do," Gilberto said.

"Then, they must realize that Kamara is jeopardizing the legitimacy of all the Guilds."

Gilberto flagged down a waiter, who walked briskly to their table.

"Espresso, please," Gilberto said. He raised two fingers and made a 'V'. "Two shots."

The waiter nodded then turned his attention to Stephen. "Anything for you, sir?"

"A glass of cranberry juice."

The waiter smiled. "I will return shortly with your drinks." He walked off.

"What the Guildmasters realize is that the Bloodmen are dealing with a personal matter that is out of control," Gilberto said. "What you did goes against all Guild protocol. Your actions are more dangerous than anything Kamara has done."

"You can't be serious," Stephen whispered, looking around as if he felt he was being watched.

The Waiter returned with their drinks. Gilberto took his time, adding several teaspoons of raw sugar and cream to his espresso before he spoke again, "Let's be candid," he said. "Kamara has made some questionable decisions, but, until recently, none of those decisions violated protocol."

"So, you admit it," Stephen said with a sly smile. "Good!"

"No, no. You misunderstand," Gilberto said, shaking his head. "While the pro bono Stanton contract is frowned upon, it does not warrant Vendetta. Letting you live after you denounced your Guild does."

Gilberto calmly took a few sips of espresso.

"You don't understand," Stephen cried. "Kamara will ruin us all."

Gilberto stared at Stephen; his face expressionless. "I understand that if you were one of my Guild brothers—a Diablo—you'd be dead."

Gilberto stood.

"Do yourself a favor, Stephen," he continued. "Go back to your Guild. Kamara will accept you back. He has a soft spot for you. If you decide to continue down this path, I suggest you disappear. The other Houses will not tolerate any more protocol violations. Enjoy your lunch."

Stephen watched Gilberto walk away. Once Gilberto sauntered out the door, he slammed his fist onto the table.

CHAPTER SEVEN

Kamara sat at the head of the long conference table in the Bloodmen's Ile. A statue of a leopard hunting various prey rested in the four corners of the room. One statue is made of onyx; one of ivory; one of copper and one statue of iron. The Bloodmen had chosen the leopard as its totem animal because, in African traditions and folklore, the Lion was not and had never been seen as the King of the Jungle. Lions lived in Savannah not the rain forests or jungles. Also, the leopard was more respected because, although it was smaller than the lion, it was much smarter.

When going lion hunting, one warrior carried a big shield and teased the lion and when it attacked, the warrior dropped to the ground and covered himself with the shield. As the lion stood there, wondering where the warrior went, the rest of the hunting party jumped on the lion and killed it.

A leopard, on the other hand, was much harder to kill because it would attack in all directions and not be distracted from its attack, this is why Africans consider the leopard to be the King of the Jungle and why African chiefs wore leopard skins instead of lion skins.

And among the guilds of assassins, the

Bloodmen were king. The elite among killers. The efficient men of blood and shadow who gave other assassins nightmares.

The leaders of the other Guilds—newly appointed Guildmaster Hideshi, of the Ronin; Guildmaster Helmut Heinrich and Guild Professor Gunter Shultz of Das Kampf; Guildmaster Kwan Li-Ming and Guild Professor Yuen Mei-Mei of Hung Gerk Kune and Guildmaster Raul Gomez of the Diablo Guild—sat around the table, listening to Guild Professor Gilberto's last words to Stephen rise from the speakers in the room's ceiling and floor. "...The other houses will not tolerate any more protocol violations. Enjoy your lunch."

"This is an unfortunate situation, Kamara," Helmut Heinrich said.

"One that must be dealt with swiftly," Guildmaster Kwan Li-Ming warned.

"Yes, of course," Kamara said. "My apologies. It seems I underestimated Stephen's anger."

"The longer you wait, the more dangerous he will become, old friend," Raul said. "We cannot afford to have Stephen expose our plans by exposing you."

Kamara nodded.

"We can't let *The Inside* get wind of our coup," Helmut said. "They have to be overthrown before they use their influence on the world's governments and the media to bring about the demise of the Guilds."

"If we can wrest control of our respective governments from within their systems, we will have the influence to stop the goals of The

Inside," Li-Ming said. "If we fail, The Inside will make slaves of us all."

Kamara took a sip of bourbon then pointed his glass toward the other guild leaders. "I will take care of this situation expeditiously," he said. "You have my word."

CHAPTER EIGHT

Senator Stanton, escorted by Chief Colby and two other Secret Service Agents, hopped out of a Mercedes Limousine and walked briskly toward the Russell Senate Office Building.

Colby and the agents closed in on the senator as reporters tried to swarm him—the agents on his flanks and Colby stood right over Stanton's right shoulder.

They paused so that the Senator could speak to the press and address the people.

"Senator Stanton," the first reporter called. When Stanton looked her way, she asked her question, "Senator Stanton, do you think it's a good idea for you to show up to work in light of the fact there is a Bloodmen contract on your head?"

"Look, I am not going to let that punk, McCarthy, dictate how I live," Senator Stanton said. "There's work to be done, so here I am."

"You seem quite jovial Senator," another reporter chimed in. "Are you taking the contract seriously?"

"Should I?" Stanton asked. He smiled. "Actually, I'm flattered that my opponents had to go to such great efforts to oppose me."

"Aren't you the least bit concerned for your life?" a third reporter asked.

"I'm concerned about what's right," the senator replied. "The Founding Fathers of this country never coerced someone in disagreement with them with the threat of death. The Assassin Guilds are constitutionally and morally wrong and I will see them eradicated." Stanton leaned closer to the reporter's microphone and stared into the camera. "If doing so means putting my life on the line, so be it!" He stepped away from the microphone and waved at the reporters as he began to walk off. "No more questions, guys. I don't want to be late on my first day back."

Chief Colby led Stanton into the building.

Stanton followed Colby toward his office. He stopped in front of the restroom.

"Hold on, I'll be back," the senator said. "Nature calls."

Colby looked at the agent on Stanton's left flank. "Go with him."

Stanton frowned. "Jesus, Chief Colby! I can piss by myself."

"Someone has to keep an eye on you, sir," Chief Colby replied.

Stanton rolled his eyes. "No! I'll be right out; damn!"

"Yes, sir," Colby said.

Colby watched him go in. The agents kept watch in the hallway in all directions.

Stanton entered the restroom alone. Inside, there was a set of urinals and four stalls. There was also a row of sinks with a mirror that ran the length of the wall. The knobs and levers on the urinals and sinks in the posh restroom were gold.

Stanton urinated and then washed his hands. He looked in the mirror and straightened his tie then opened the restroom door to leave.

A man dressed in a black, skin-tight jumpsuit, pulled Stanton back into the restroom and held a knife to his throat as the man pressed Stanton's back against the sink. The man's face was concealed by a black balaclava.

"It can happen this fast, Senator Stanton," the man whispered. "That's how good the Bloodmen are."

"Who... who are you?" Stanton croaked. "How did you... where's Chief Colby? The... the Secret Service...?"

"Don't panic," the man said. "I am not here to kill you. We need to meet. Any questions you have will be answered then. Now turn and face the mirror."

"Hell no!"

The man spun Stanton around effortlessly and shoved his face against the mirror.

You're brave. I'll give you that," the man in black said. "Count to ten before you turn around."

"One...two...three...four—" Stanton counted.

Stanton whirled around and snatched the restroom door open.

The man was nowhere to be seen.

Chief Colby and the Secret Service Agents were lying unconscious on the floor.

"Chief Colby? Chief Colby?" Senator Stanton shouted.

Chief Colby and the Agents began to stir. Colby moaned as he struggled to his feet.

"What happened?" Colby moaned. "We—"

"It was an assassin, I think," the senator chimed in. "But he didn't work for the Bloodmen. He wants to meet, but he didn't tell me where."

Chief Colby opened his fist, revealing a flash drive in his hand.

"I think he did," Colby said.

Stanton took the flash drive and put it in his pocket.

"What are you going to do, sir?" Chief Colby asked.

"I'll see what's on this flash drive and then I'll decide," Stanton replied.

The man in black stood against the door with his ear pressed to it, listening to Stanton and Colby's conversation. He removed the mask, revealing Stephen's smiling face.

CHAPTER NINE

In a nondescript neighborhood, a moderately-sized brick house sat. Inside, was a group of young men and women who, like many around the world, idolized the Assassin Guilds. This particular group was called the Tigers and their favorite guild of assassins was the Bloodmen.

The Tigers were having a good time—shooting pool on a dilapidated table; making out on ragged couches and chairs; eating ramen noodles and drinking grape soda as they joked around.

The front door swung open and Stephen sauntered inside. The Tigers sprang to their feet, staring down the stranger in their midst.

"You took one hell of a wrong turn, old dude," a Tiger said, pointing the end of his pool cue at Stephen.

Stephen calmly looked around, as if admiring his new home.

"No, I'm exactly where I want to be," he said. "I must say, I'm disappointed, though. I expected more from a gang of Bloodmen wannabees."

"Wrong answer, bruh!" the Tiger with the pool cue spat.

The Tiger charged; his pool cue held over his shoulder. He swung.

Stephen evaded the blow then crouched and swept the young man off his feet with a lightning fast kick to his Achilles tendon.

Stephen stood, brushing a wrinkle out of his sweater.

"Like I said...disappointed."

All the Tigers in the room attacked.

Stephen was like water, flowing through his attackers with perfect technique—every strike a strong tide; every throw a crashing wave. He was a master among beginners.

The door to a room with an engraved plaque above it that read, "Throne Room," opened. An athletically built young man with a short afro, twisted into thin coils, stepped out. He was dressed like his brethren—in black tactical boots, gray camouflage pants, and a t-shirt with "TIGERS" stenciled in white letters across the back.

"What the hell is going on?" the young man shouted. When he spotted Stephen, his eyes widened in recognition.

"Shit!" he yelled, charging toward the fray.

He began snatching Tigers and throwing them onto couches and into walls.

"Stop it!" the man ordered. "Stop it, god damn it! Don't you fools know who this is?"

The Tigers ceased fighting, expressions of confusion on their faces.

Carlos stood before Stephen then knelt and assumed the traditional salute of the Bloodmen. The rest of the Tigers exchanged glances then followed suit. Stephen knelt and returned the salute.

They stood and the young man extended his hand toward Stephen. The former Guild Professor shook it.

I'm so sorry, Professor," the young man said. "My Tigers didn't know who you are. It's my fault."

"It's okay," Stephen said. "It was a good workout. So, you're Carlos Fairchild."

"Yes," Carlos said, beaming with pride. "Yes, I am, Professor!"

"I've heard great things about your operation," Stephen said, looking around. "It's good to finally meet you."

Carlos took Stephen's hand again and kissed it. Stephen snatched his hand away, frowning.

"The hell?" Stephen said.

Carlos lowered his gaze, embarrassed. "Oh, I'm so sorry. Isn't that a traditional African salute?"

"Africa is a big place," Stephen said. "But if you mean the Wolof salute, you place your forehead to the back of the hand, not your lips."

"It's just... well... I never expected to see a real Bloodman in my spot, let alone a Professor," Carlos said. "Pardon my ignorance, but why are you here?"

"Good question," Stephen said. "Where can we talk?"

"Follow me, Professor," Stephen said, walking toward the "Throne Room" door.

Carlos led Stephen into his "Throne

Room." Unlike the outer room, this room was actually aesthetically beautiful. It was set up like a living room in a mansion, with expensive furniture and an authentic golden stool—a throne from the Akan people of Ghana, West Africa. Stephen sat on the throne. Carlos sat in a leather swivel chair opposite him.

"Would you like anything to drink?" Carlos asked. "Water? Patron? Moscato? A smoothie?"

"No, I'm fine," Stephen said, studying the posh room. "You seem to be doing quite well here, Carlos."

"We do okay, Professor."

"So, how do you manage to do so... 'okay'?"

"We take on protection contracts," Carlos replied. "No assassinations, of course. At least, not yet. I've applied for Guild Certification and Licensing several times, but each time we're refused.

"Trying to give the Bloodmen some competition, huh?" Stephen said with a slight smile.

"Of course not, Professor," Carlos said. "We don't have any delusions here. We would love to be Bloodmen, but we know that's not possible."

Stephen leaned forward in his chair. "What if I told you that it is?"

Carlos' eyes widened. "What?"

"This is an opportunity for every last one of you to become Bloodmen," Stephen replied. "But not like the Bloodmen you know. A better class of assassin; far beyond what you admire and aspire to be."

"How is that possible?" Carlos asked.

"You know of Guildmaster Kamara Keita, yes?"

"Of course!" Carlos said.

"Kamara has proven to be an excellent Oluwo," Stephen said. "But recently, he put the Bloodmen on a path that could destroy every Guild in existence. I've left the Bloodmen because of his rash and dangerous decisions."

"You quit?" Carlos said, shocked. "You gave up being a Bloodman? How? Why?"

"I could no longer stomach the corruption surrounding me," Stephen said. "I appealed to the other Guilds, but they refused to listen; so I came here, hoping to find a new beginning among the uncorrupt."

Stephen stared at Carlos, his eyes cold.

"Kamara needs to be stopped before he destroys us all," he said. "I can't do it alone though. I need your help, Carlos."

"Our help? I don't know Professor. The Tigers are nowhere near as good as the Bloodmen."

"You can be; under my tutelage," Stephen said. "Besides, what we need to accomplish our goals goes beyond training."

"What do you mean, Professor?"

"We need weapons, Carlos; and I need people who know how to use them and use them well."

Carlos hopped to his feet and paced the floor.

"Forgive me, Professor, but this is confusing to me," Carlos said. "You come to our sanctuary; offer to make the Tigers Bloodmen; and then you ask us to wage an illegal Vendetta against the very Guild we respect the most? I don't know, Professor."

"Extraordinary challenges require extraordinary solutions," Stephen said. "I know this challenges all you believe about the Bloodmen. I wish there was some other way to deal with Kamara, but there isn't."

"If we go after the Bloodmen with firearms, the cops will have our asses," Carlos said.

"That will be taken care of," Stephen said. "Believe me."

"I'm not sure about all of this," Carlos said, shaking his head.

Stephen rose from the throne.

"I'm sorry I wasted your time, Carlos," Stephen said. "I thought I had come to the right man for this. I was wrong."

Stephen sauntered out of the throne room and exited the house. He slowly walked to his car.

Carlos ran outside.

"Professor, wait," he called.

A sly smile spreads across Stephen's face. He changed his expression to a serious one before he turned to face Carlos.

"Our business is finished, Carlos."

"No, Professor," Carlos cried. "I mean... forgive me. We *will* help you. Whatever you want... we'll do it!"

Stephen approached Carlos and placed a huge hand on the young man's shoulder.

"Thank you, Carlos," he said. "I know

this is a hard decision for you. You will not regret this."

"What do you need us to do, Professor?"

"Gather the necessary weapons and personnel," Stephen said. "I have a few details to take care of."

Stephen climbed into a candy apple red mid-size SUV.

"We'll get right on it, Professor," Carlos said. "When will I hear from you?"

Stephen started the vehicle's engine.

"Soon, Carlos," Stephen replied. "Very soon."

CHAPTER TEN

The Bloodmen gathered in the grand Banquet Hall of their Ile, standing along the walls, mingling, or relaxing in a plush leather chair at one of the circular, granite tables in the room.

On the walls of the capacious room were weapons and shields from all over Africa.

The Bloodmen were dressed in their formal regalia—a long-sleeve indigo tunic and matching trousers with a brown leather vest over the tunic. The vest was covered in columns of cowries and rows of small juju bags.

The Guildmasters and Guild Professors from the other Guilds were also present, sitting in high-back leather chairs in a roped off section, enjoying the best bourbon, whiskey, wine, or liqueur the world had to offer.

Kamara—dressed in the same regalia as his students, but his clothing was white and his leather vest was indigo—worked his way through the crowd, stately and confident in appearance and manner. He finally made his way to the VIP section and the Guildmasters.

"Danke schon, for inviting us, Kamara," Helmut said. "I had forgotten what a fine Guildhouse you have."

"The finest," Kamara said with a smile. "But we all think that of our houses, I'm sure."

"Si," Raul agreed. "Too fine a house to be brought down by indecision."

"Mein Gott, Raul," Helmut said. "We're guests."

"No, he's fine, Helmut," Kamara said. He turned to Raul. "Speak your mind."

"You have not taken care of Stephen Jones," Raul said. "If you cannot, or *will* not, then admit your weakness and we will deal with him before it's too late."

"Raul makes a valid point," Li-Ming chimed in.

"Perhaps," Kamara said. "But tonight, is not about business, esteemed Guildmasters. Tonight, is about honoring our ancestors."

Kamara waved his hand and drummers began playing. Beautiful African dancers and stilt walkers followed and everything became more alive.

"Enjoy yourselves, Masters," Kamara said. "And thank you, again, for attending."

Kamara walked away from the master assassins and joined in with the dancing crowd.

CHAPTER ELEVEN

Jamela sat in the lobby of *Xkalibur Atlanta*—dubbed the newest, funkiest posh hotel in the world by *Hospitality Magazine*. A white man in his mid-forties eyed Jamela admiringly, not worried about his wife catching his wandering eyes as she was too busy trying to rein in their pair of sons, who were running around the lobby, bumping into guests and wrestling with each other.

"Parker... Wesley... settle down or you'll get a time out," she threatened.

"Time out?" the man said, exhaling a quick breath. "Their asses need time *in*... jail. Brats!"

Jamela looks in the man's direction. He winked at her. Jamela rolled her eyes. The man pulled a wad of money out of his pocket and handed it to his wife.

"Sweetheart, go get the kids a smoothie," he said. "That should settle them down. Get something for yourself, too. Oh, and grab me a mocha latte. I just love the mocha lattes they serve here."

He flashed Jamela a sly look and licked his lips.

Jamela shook her head.

The man's wife snatched up the children and left the lobby.

The man slithered over to Jamela and took a seat beside her.

"Hello, beautiful," he said. "My name's James; James Daniels and you are?"

"Mocha latte?" she said, shaking her head. "For real? Come on, now, James."

"It's true," James said. "I see you... I think 'mocha latte'."

"And when you see your wife?"

"I think *not* mocha latte," James said. "So, what's your name, beautiful?"

Jamela reached in the pocket of her jacket and pulled out a business card. She handed it to James.

James read the card aloud— "Jamela... pretty name... Jamela Rashon... Bloodman Assassin?"

James looked as if he had seen a ghost. He looked up at Jamela wide-eyed.

Jamela formed her fingers into the shape of a gun and gestured like she was shooting him.

"Bang!" Jamela blurted out.

James jumped and scurried back to his seat.

Jamela's taxi pulled up in the driveway.

She smiled. "Perfect timing."

* * *

Malcolm stood on the Marta platform, awaiting the train from the airport to downtown. He looked down at the titanium bracer on his right forearm and checked his Vidcomm. The wallpaper on the screen was a photo of him with Jamela, who was making a funny face. He smiled at the picture. The screenplay shifted to show the time was 1930 Hours.

Malcolm looked up and noticed a menacing-looking man dressed in a black hoodie, blue jeans and shell-toe sneakers watching him. He perused the platform and spotted three more men spying him.

The train arrived. Malcolm hopped on it. The men spying him entered the train also.

Malcolm rode the train for a few stops and then he darted through the opening doors. The men scrambled off the train behind him. Malcolm sprinted out of the station and the men gave chase. He led them to a secluded area on the side of a factory that was closed for the night and then he suddenly turned and approached them.

"What do you want with me, brothers?" Malcolm asked. "If this is a robbery, I would advise you to seek a target that comes with less... consequences."

"This ain't no robbery, Bloodman," the menacing man in the hoodie said. "We've come to collect something from you."

"Which is?" Malcolm asked.

"Your heart," the hoodie-wearing thug answered.

"No can do," Malcolm said, patting his chest. "It already belongs to someone else; but don't worry, there's somebody out there for everybody... even your ugly ass."

The corners of the lips of the man in the hoodie rose into a twisted smile.

"You're real funny," he said. "But you're right. There *is* somebody out there for me. That ho' you was gonna get married to. After we're done with you, I'm gon' go have some fun with her... before I skin the bitch alive!"

Malcolm's face twisted into a mask of anger and he rushed forward on the attack.

* * *

Jamela sat in the back of the cab, looking out the window at a city she had not visited in over two years.

"We're a couple of blocks from the Bloodmen's guild house, Ms. Rashon," the man said. "Please don't forget to put in the good word for my boy, Rodney. He'll be out of the Marines soon and he'll be needing something to do."

"I got you, hun," Jamela said, patting the driver's headrest. "If Rodney can make it through the rigorous selection process and the training, he'll be a Bloodman in no time."

Two black vans whizzed past the cab.

"Assholes!"

Jamela sensed something was wrong.

"Let me out here," she said. "I'll walk the rest of the way."

"Are you sure?" the cabbie asked.

"Positive," Jamela replied.

The cabbie pulled over to the curb. Jamela handed him a hundred-dollar bill.

"Keep the change," she said, sliding out of the car. "Drop off my luggage tomorrow morning."

"Wow! Thanks!" the cabbie said, smiling broadly. "Well, talk to you tomorrow, Ms. Rashon. Thanks, again, for Rodney."

"No problem, hun," she said as she turned away from the taxi. "Bye."

Jamela jogged toward the Ile.

"Damn," she sighed. "Malcolm... Papa... please be okay."

She sped up to a sprint when she heard gunfire.

***

Malcolm squared off with the thugs, who had all drawn weapons—the thug in the black hoodie was armed with a hatchet; two other men wielded tactical knives and a fourth wielded a bowie knife the size of a machete.

Titanium louvers slid over the vidcomm's screen on Malcolm's arm, forming a protective bracer.

One of the tactical knife-wielding thugs smiled, baring his gold incisors, then thrust his knife toward Malcolm's gut.

Malcolm blocked the thrust with the back of both of his forearms then grabbed the gold-toothed thug's arm and yanked it to off balance him.

The gold-toothed man stumbled toward Malcolm.

Malcolm slammed the titanium-covered vid-comm into the man's face. A loud KRAAK exploded from the thug's pulverized nose and upper teeth.

The thug fell to the ground, his face smashed in beyond recognition. A gold tooth lay in a pool of blood by his head.

The mountain of a man with the big bowie knife was surprisingly fast for his size. He exploded forward, slashing furiously at Malcolm's face.

Malcolm evaded the slashes with side-steps and quick slips of his shoulder.

The other man with the tactical knife rushed toward Malcolm.

Malcolm halted the thug's charge with a downward kick to the knife-wielding thug's knee. His lower leg collapsed inward with a SNAP. The thug fell to the ground, screaming in agony.

The big man with the big bowie knife slashed again. Malcolm blocked it with the vid-comm then grabbed the big man's wrist, whirled about and slammed the big thug's elbow down onto the top of his shoulder, dislocating the thug's elbow.

The hoodie-wearing man charged toward Malcolm.

Malcolm released the mountainous man's wrist and he is fell behind Malcolm, a look of agony on his face, Malcolm reached out for the Bowie knife falling in front of him.

Malcolm caught the bowie knife's handle.

The hoodie-wearing thug slashed his hatchet at Malcolm's head.

Malcolm lowered his stance and the hatchet's blade flew over his head. Malcolm stabbed the Bowie knife through the hoodie-wearing thug's outer thigh. It tore through his trousers and jutted through the inside of his leg.

The thug wailed.

Malcolm grabbed the thug's hatchet-wielding wrist with one hand and the knife in his leg with the other the shoved the man against a wall.

"Who sent you?" Malcolm asked. "Is this Vendetta?"

"Fuck you!" the man shouted. "I ain't saying shit!"

Malcolm pushed the knife deeper into the thug's flesh, toward the back of his thigh. Blood ran down the man's leg on the outside and inside of his trousers.

"I will carve out every muscle... every bone... if you don't tell me what I want to know," Malcolm said. He locked eyes with the thug. "You understand me?"

Malcolm pushed on the knife as he held the hatchet against the wall.

The thug's face contorted in pain. "Aaah! O-okay... please... no more," the man cried. "I'll talk. You really don't know what kind of shit you're in, do you?"

"Tell me."

"This ain't no Vendetta," the hoodie-wearing man said. "It's bigger than that. Global big. Yo' Daddy pissed off the wrong mu-hfuckas!"

"Who?" Malcolm said. "Speak!"

"The muhfuckin'—"

Blood sprayed from Malcolm's back and the hoodie-wearing man's eyes rolled toward the back of his skull as his head was thrown backward.

Malcolm fell on his face, a bloody hole in the middle of his back, just to the side of his spine.

The thug lay dead with a hole in the center of his chest.

On a rooftop, Carlos held a *Mauser 18* hunting rifle. The barrel of the rifle was still smoking. Carlos pressed an ear-bud that was in his ear as he looked down at Malcolm and the thugs as they lay on the ground.

"The son has been neutralized, sir," he said.

Stephen's voice came from the ear-bud. "Excellent. Get to the Guild-house immediately!"

"Yes, sir," Carlos said.

Carlos rested his rifle on his shoulder and ran to the door leading from the roof.

CHAPTER TWELVE

Jamela turned the corner and the Ile was in view. The black vans were parked outside of it. The doors slid open and men and women poured out of each van. They were dressed in black military gear and are armed with assault rifles. On the back of their tactical vests was stenciled 'Tigers' in white letters.

"What the hell? Jamela whispered. "Vendetta? No one told me!"

A Tiger came back outside and began dragging a box out of the van.

Jamela quickly snuck up on him.

"Pardon me, asshole army-dude," Jamela said sweetly.

The man whirled around. Jamela slammed the space between her thumb and index finger into his throat. She caught the *Steyr AUG* assault rifle that fell from his lifeless fingers, turned and ran toward the guild house.

Jamela charged into the house, firing the assault rifle and killing several Tigers and their thug cohorts. Her eyes widened and her jaw fell slack when she noticed the massacre of Bloodmen, whose corpses lay everywhere.

The few left alive were fighting, but they had lost; overwhelmed by the vicious surprise attack by the Tigers and thugs.

Jamela continued to creep through the guild house. She discovered several dead Guildmasters and Guild Professors. A critically injured Kamara staggered out of the shadows.

Startled, Jamela pointed the rifle at him. Upon recognizing her leader and father-figure, she dropped the weapon and ran to him, catching him just as he collapsed.

"Papa!" she cried. "Oh, Papa, no!"

"Go Diaspora, Jamela," Kamara said weakly. "Find Malcolm. Tell him... tell him the Bloodmen are no more!"

Tears ran down Jamela's cheeks.

"Don't talk like that, Papa," she cried. "I'm gonna get you help. You're gonna be okay."

"I'm finished, baby," Kamara croaked. "Malcolm never made it here. Find him. Go Diaspora!"

"I'm not leaving you, Papa. We're gonna get you help!"

Stephen ran into the room. He wore the same black military uniform as the Tigers. He saw Jamela with Kamara and smiled. Jamela looked up and Stephen changed his smile to a look of concern.

"Is Oluwo Kamara okay?" he asked.

"Stephen! Thank God!" Jamela sighed. "If we hurry, I think he'll live."

Stephen smiled.

Jamela studied him. She noticed that he was not injured at all, nor was there blood on him and he was not wearing the uniform of a Bloodman.

"Stephen?" Jamela said, looking at Stephen confused. "You—"

"You're smarter than you act, little sister," Stephen said.

Jamela gently laid Kamara on the floor.

"Hold on, Papa," she said to Kamara. "Hold on, you hear me?"

"Jamela, no!" Kamara said. "Go Diaspora! Run!"

Jamela stood and raised her fists.

"Defiant as ever," Steven said, smiling. "You should have followed your Oluwo's orders and ran."

"Traitor!" Jamela spat. "How could you do this? The other Guilds are—"

The other Guilds have fallen," Stephen said. "There are no Guilds... except for the one I control."

Jamela pointed at Stephen and said, "I'm gonna kill you, you treacherous little bitch!"

Stephen glared at Jamela. "I am going to rip out your disrespectful little tongue!"

Stephen leapt at Jamela. She charged toward him.

Stephen launched a round kick at Jamela's head.

Jamela blocked the blow with a raised elbow and the palm of her other hand.

Jamela hit Stephen in the chin with an upward elbow. His head snapped backward from the force.

Stephen slammed a knee into Jamela's

gut. She vomited a gust of air.

Stephen slapped Jamela hard in the face. Jamela's staggered sideways from the blow. Tigers and thugs ran into the room, guns raised. They started shooting.

Jamela dove behind a table for cover.

She darted out of the Banquet Hall with bullets flying behind her.

Stephen raised his powerful arms, yelling, "Stop!"

The Tigers and thugs lowered their weapons.

Stephen glared at them. "Fools! Never interrupt me when I'm killing someone!"

Stephen grabbed a thug and twisted his neck until his chin rested between his shoulder blades.

Suddenly, an expression of calm came over Stephen. He inhaled deeply, closing his eyes and savoring the kill.

"Find the girl and bring her back to me!"

The men and women filed out of the room.

Stephen heard Kamara cough up blood. He turned toward his former Master and smiled.

"And now, Oluwo, it's time for you to submit your resignation."

He sauntered toward Kamara.

CHAPTER THIRTEEN

Five years later. . .

It was a typically hot and dry day in Matamoros, Tamaulipas State, Mexico. The *Sand Dollar Motel* was worn down and sparsely populated. A toothless old woman sat outside her motel room in a rocking chair. A couple of dusty, shoeless children played with a scruffy dog and a man slept with his back against a tree.

Inside one of the motel's rooms, a woman with a beautiful, athletic body and smooth, brown skin lay face down on a made bed. She wore only a bra and panties.

A wind-up alarm clock went off. The woman smacked the clock off the night-stand. She lifted her head slowly then groaned. Her hair was disheveled, but she was still beautiful. She sniffed her armpit and frowned.

Jamela dragged herself out of bed and trudged to the bathroom, clumsily taking off her bra and panties along the way. She took a quick shower, which invigorated her. Jamela hopped out of the shower and strode to the dresser. She opened the top drawer. Two pistols lay on top of her underwear and waitress uniform. She dressed quickly, grabbed her purse and keys and exited the room.

On the breezeway, Jamela turned a corner and came face to face with a sleazy, greasy man in his early forties. The man smiled, exposing a golden grill.

"Good morning, Mocha," he said.

"Fuck you, Smitty!" Jamela hissed.

"I see we're on the same page," Smitty said, looking her up and down.

Jamela rolled her eyes, pushed past Smitty and began walking away.

"You know rent is due tomorrow," he said.

"Don't worry, I'll have it, she said.

"You know, paying the rent ain't always got to be about money," he said.

"With your nasty ass, it's always about money," she said.

Jamela turned away from Smitty and ran down the metal stairs, which led to the parking lot. She jumped into an old *Mustang GT* and burned rubber as she sped away.

* * *

Jamela pulled into the lot of Munchie's Café, a triple-wide mobile home, turned greasy-spoon restaurant. She jumped out of her car and trotted to the door. She took a deep breath and went in.

An overweight Mexican man in his early fifties stood behind the counter serving breakfast and coffee to a restaurant full of truckers and locals. Everyone looked toward the door and smiled when they saw Jamela.

"Mocha!" everyone said in unison.

"Morning honeys and honettes!" Jamela said, smiling broadly.

She ran behind the counter. The pudgy man frowned at her.

"You're late, again, Mocha," he said.

Jamela kissed the man on the cheek. "Sorry, mi padre mayor."

"Whatever," the man said.

"Come on, Munchie," Jamela said, giving him a big hug. "Stop acting mad. You know you love me."

"Alright, alright," Munchie said, nudging her away. "Get your ass to work! You're on my time—"

"And my dime!" The patrons said with Munchie.

Everyone laughed.

Jamela grabbed her order book and apron. She turned to work the floor when she saw two black Lincoln *Town Cars* pull up to the front of the diner. Men in black suits and sunglasses emerged from the cars. They were obviously government types. Jamela guessed *Policía Federal.*

The PF agents perused the surrounding area.

Jamela turned her back to the door then quickly approached the kitchen.

"Hey, Munchie," Jamela said to the pudgy man. "I'll be back. I gotta check something in the kitchen."

Jamela walked through the swinging doors of the kitchen then ripped off her apron and headed for the back door. She froze when she saw a car pull up to the rear of the restaurant. Two officers got out.

Jamela plopped down hard on her butt to keep them from seeing her.

"Shit! Shit! Shit!" she whispered.

She looked around quickly, spotting a couple of knives on a counter. She scooted to the counter, reached up and grabbed two knives—a small steak knife and a large butcher knife.

Back in the dining area, the officers entered the restaurant. Munchie approached them.

"Welcome to Munchie's Café," he said with a smile. "How may I help you?"

One agent, a white man in his mid-forties, with salt-and-pepper hair, removed his Oakley sunglasses and slipped them into the breast pocket of his suit jacket. "I'm Special Agent Jesus Calderon, *Policía Federal*," he said, holding up his badge and identification card. "We're looking for a fugitive whom wc have reason to believe works here. Have you seen this woman?

He put away his badge then handed Munchie a photograph. It was a picture of a slightly younger Jamela. Munchie handed the photo back to Morrison.

"Never seen her before."

"Mind if we look around?" Morrison asked.

"You got a warrant?" Munchie asked.

The officers exchanged glances and smiles.

"People usually ask if we have a warrant

if they have something to hide," Calderon said. "Do you have something . . . or someone to hide, Dumpy?"

"That's Munchie," Munchie said. "Go ahead; search all you like."

"Thanks, Lard Ass," Jesus said. "Did I say it right that time?"

The Marshals laughed.

Munchie raised his middle finger.

The Marshals searched the dining area, studying each customer carefully. A few checked the restrooms. They returned shaking their heads.

"I guess the kitchen is next, huh?" Munchie said loudly.

"Please, Humpty, don't try to tell us how to do—"

Morrison's expression changed to one of realization as it became clear to him what Munchie was trying to do.

"The kitchen. Now!" Calderon ordered.

The officers scrambled into the kitchen. It appeared to be empty. They fanned out, weapons drawn, searching for her.

Suddenly, Jamela sprang up and slit one of the officer's wrist with the steak knife, causing him to drop his weapon. She spun and hurled the steak knife at another officer as he fired his gun. She ducked and a bullet just missed her. The steak knife lodged in the officer's eye. He fell, lifeless, onto his back.

Back in the dining area, the customers ran out of the store in a panic as more shots and men's screams rang out from the kitchen.

Munchie charged into the kitchen.

"Mocha? Mocha, are you alright?" he asked.

Munchie spotted Jamela crouching behind a counter. He saw the bloody butcher knife in Jamela's hand. He looked down and saw Special Agent Morrison at Jamela's feet, riddled with knife wounds then he looked around and saw a dead officer with a knife protruding from his eye and another lying dead in a pool of blood.

Munchie's eyes widened in shock.

"Mocha?" Munchie said, staring at her.

"Munchie, get out of here," she whispered. "Now!"

The back door burst open. Two officers charged in, guns blazing.

Munchie scrambled back into the dining area as Jamela dove for Calderon's pistol a yard away. Bullets tore holes in the floor where she just crouched.

Jamela grabbed the gun, rolled to her feet and shot one of the officers twice in the chest. He staggered backward into the rear wall then slid down it, falling lifeless onto his haunches. His head slumped forward and a stream of bloody drool poured from his mouth into his lap.

The other officer fired, but his pistol was empty. He whirled about and darted out the back door.

"No, the hell you don't," Jamela shouted.

She aimed at the Marshal's back and pulls the trigger, but Calderon's gun was also empty.

"Shit," Jamela said, jumping over the counter. She took off after the officer.

Outside, she perused the area until she spotted the officer in his car.

The officer gunned the engine and sped toward her.

Jamela charged toward the car.

The officer sped up even more.

Jamela leapt to the side to evade the car while simultaneously hurling the empty pistol at officer's forehead.

The gun flew through the lowered window and struck the officer in the temple, dazing him.

The officer crashed his car into the rear wall of the restaurant. He flew through the windshield and his head slammed into the wall. He collapses onto the hood of his car, twitched a few times and then lay still.

Munchie ran around to the rear of the restaurant.

"M'hija, what the hell is going on?" he asked.

"I'm sorry, Munchie, but I can't tell you," Jamela said. "The less you know, the better, amigo."

"Can I help?"

"No, Papi," Jamela replied. "If more officers show up and they even think you're helping me, they'll kill you. If more come and they question you, tell them the truth. Thanks, for everything, Munchie."

Jamela turned away from Munchie and sprinted around the front of the restaurant to her car. She hopped in and sped off, leaving a cloud of dust.

* * *

Jamela pulled into the parking lot of the motel. She hopped out of her car and ran up the stairs to the second-floor breezeway then sprinted to her room. She opened the door.

Inside the room Smitty sat at the foot of her bed, watching national news on her television.

"Back so soon?" Smitty asked.

Jamela walked past Smitty and began to pack the items in the dresser into a duffle bag.

"Get the fuck out of my room," she said, not looking at Smitty.

"Oh, you're acting all funny now that you're a celebrity, huh?" Smitty said.

"A celebrity? What have you been smokin'?"

"Yeah, a celebrity," Smitty said." You've been all over the news. An armed and danger- ous fugitive, huh? Well, your secret's safe with me, baby... provided you give me a little pussy every now and then for my troubles."

Jamela's eyes grew wide and her face shifted from initial disbelief to fury. She continued to pack.

"What?" she said.

Smitty stood then turned to face Jamela. He grabbed his groin.

"I said, I promise not to call the feds if you give me a little puss—"

Jamela shot Smitty twice in the chest— once with each pistol. She then calmly placed the guns into her waistband. She searched Smitty's corpse until she found the keys to his pickup truck and his wallet, which had a few hundred-dollar bills stuffed into it.

"Hey, Smitty, mind if I borrow your car?"

Jamela stared into Smitty's lifeless eyes, as if she was really awaiting an answer.

"I didn't think so."

She snatched the keys and headed toward the door, but she was stopped in her tracks by a news report on the television.

"In other news," the anchor woman went on. "President Stanton visited Toronto to meet with Canadian Prime Minister, Estelle Butler about Canada's continued and increasing problems with domestic terrorism. President Stanton was accompanied by Director of the CIA, Carlos Fairchild and newly appointed Secretary of Defense, Stephen Jones."

Jamela's head jerked back toward the television screen at the mention of Stephen's name.

"The fuck?"

On the television screen, Stanton walked with Prime Minister Butler. They were flanked by Carlos and Stephen.

Jamela focused on Stephen's face. She screamed and kicked the television off its stand. The television hit the floor and the screen shattered. She turned and stormed out the door.

CHAPTER FOURTEEN

A man and a woman hiked down a trail. The snow-capped Canadian Rockies loomed behind them and to their right flank. They lowered their heads against the strong wind but when the man looked up, he revealed that he was the former Bloodman, Malcolm, but now his beard was thick and his once well-groomed afro had grown wild.

The woman with him was a Nipissing indigenous woman; pretty, but hard—like she had worked outside all her life. She was athletically built, with long black hair and light brown skin.

They both wore rain jackets over a padded insulating layer, rain pants and hiking boots.

"Did you find it this time?" the woman asked.

"Find what, Jenny?"

"Whatever you're looking for in those mountains, Malcolm," she replied. "I mean, you're up there every day, you must be looking for something."

"Yeah... peace and quiet."

"The only way you'll get more peace and quiet than in this sleepy town is if you're dead."

"Well, I'm just glad I finally got you to walk with me, Ms. Running-Fox."

"Well, I didn't have any clients to see today," she said. "So, I figured I'd spend the day with my favorite person in town."

"Shouldn't your husband be your favorite?" Malcolm said with a smirk.

"My favorite asshole, maybe," she replied. "Look, don't even get me started."

"Where is he anyway?"

"On the road, as always," she said, shaking her head.

They approached a house. A cozy place at the foot of the mountain.

"So, do you have any food in there or do we need to go to the store?" Jenny asked. "I'm fixing breakfast."

"I have food," Malcolm said. "Jenny... are you ever concerned about what people around here might think?"

Jenny stared at him.

"What? About you and me?" she said.

"Yeah," he said, unlocking the front door of the house. "This is a small town. People talk."

"Not about me," she said. "Nobody messes with a Medicine Priest. They're afraid their dicks or tits will shrivel up and fall off if I get pissed. Besides, everybody hates my husband... including me."

Malcolm shook his head and opened the door.

They entered. Taking off their jackets and insulating layers and hanging them on the wooden coat rack that stood just beyond the door.

Malcolm plopped down on the couch in the living room and used the remote to turn on the television. Jenny headed into the kitchen.

She pulled tomatoes from the refrigerator.

"Anyway, it's not like you've made a move on me, yet," she said.

Malcolm peeked into the kitchen and admired Jenny's body as she bent over, pulling a skillet and cooking utensils from under the sink.

"All this sexiness and you don't even take advantage of it," she said, placing the skillet on the stove. "You just stare at it when you think I don't notice, like you're doing now."

She looked over her shoulder and smiled slyly.

Malcolm snapped his head toward the television.

Jenny giggled.

He looked back in her direction.

"I'd be lying to say I don't want you," he said. "But I don't mess with another man's woman."

"I know. I know," she said. "Code of the Warrior and all that." She sighed. "That's part of what makes you so adorable, though."

Jenny began chopping up the tomatoes. Malcolm looked at the television. The same news report that so inflamed Jamela was on the screen.

"...about Canada's continued and increasing problems with domestic terrorism," the news anchor said. "President Stanton was accompanied by Director of the CIA, Carlos Fairchild and newly appointed Secretary of Defense, Stephen Jones."

Malcolm rose from the couch and walked to his bedroom.

He rummaged through his chest of drawers and began packing clothes into a suitcase. He opened the closet door, revealing a small safe. He typed in a code on the safe's keypad, opened it and removed a wad of hundred-dollar bills. He stuffed it into his pants pocket. When he turned around, Jenny was standing in the doorway, smiling.

"Did you change your mind? Am I gonna finally get some after all?" she asked.

"I'm gonna have to leave town," he said. "Something's come up."

"Something's come up? Like what?" she asked.

"It's personal," Malcolm said. "I'll be back in a few days. I promise."

"Then take me with you," Jenny said. "I can clear my schedule."

Malcolm shook his head. "Naw, Jen. I have to do this alone."

"Baby, please don't do this," Jenny said. "Don't put me in this position."

"I'm sorry," Malcolm said. "I... wait... what position? What are you—?"

Jenny drew a pistol from her waistband and aimed it at Malcolm.

"Who do you work for?" Malcolm asked.

"For people that want to keep tabs on

your whereabouts."

"Then you know who I am... what I was," Malcolm said.

"Not exactly," Jenny said. "I just know that you're dangerous to some very important people and they don't want you roaming about unsupervised."

"Jenny... don't do this," Malcolm said softly. "You love me... right?"

"Yeah, I really do, Malcolm," she said. "Stay here. We can be happy together."

"So, the husband is just a cover?"

"Yep, he's my handler," Jenny said. "A total asshole, like I said."

"Then I could have got some a long time ago."

"Exactly," Jenny said. She glanced at the bed then back at Malcolm. "No time like the present, though."

Malcolm smiled at Jenny seductively.

"The things I'm gonna do to you!" he said, looking her up and down.

Jenny lowered the pistol a little.

"Now, you're talking," Jenny said. "Baby we can—"

Malcolm exploded forward and struck Jenny in the temple with a palm strike. The pistol fell to the floor and Jenny collapsed into his arms, unconscious. Malcolm lowered her gently onto his bed. He kissed her softly on the lips.

"Sorry, baby. Sweet dreams."

Malcolm grabbed his bag and quickly walked out the door.

CHAPTER FIFTEEN

President Stanton walked the halls of the new White House. He looked out the window—the kudzu that crept up the oak trees was still very green even though it was an exceptionally cool Fall in Atlanta.

The president was accompanied by Carlos and a woman with smooth alabaster skin, probably the result of extensive plastic surgery, and hair that matched her crimson dress and the bottoms of her pumps.

"How was the Canadian trip?" the woman asked.

"Overall, it was good," Stanton said. "But Prime Minister Butler won't budge on the One World Government issue."

"Then Canada will experience her first and last ass-whooping at the hands of the United States of America," the woman said. "We should have torn them a new one when they refused to join the OWG fifty years ago."

"Canada has always been a friend to us, Sarah," President Stanton said. "And Estelle Butler is my friend. I am not going to war against her."

Sarah smiled slightly at the president.

"You will go where I say you go," she said. "Don't forget who your real friends are,

Patrick. The same friends who put you in the President's seat."

"I haven't forgotten," Stanton said. "It was Carlos here... and Stephen Jones. They protected me from the Bloodmen and helped me to eradicate those god-forsaken Guilds. The Guilds that your precious secret society feared. You should be grateful!"

"You were once one of us, Patrick," Sarah said. "As has been every President, Prime Minister, King, Pope, Rabbi and Grand Mufti before you. You should be grateful that we've tolerated your insolence this long! You will call for war on Canada, Mr. President, or Nigel Roth will be giving his inauguration speech come January."

Stanton stopped walking. He turned to face Sarah. "You think you can replace me with Roth?" he said. "As a Vice President, he's about as useful as a hangnail."

"He's loyal to the pursuits of the Inside," Sarah said.

"All of you baby-eating, fake witchcraft-doing, black robe-wearing bitches and sons of bitches can kiss my ass!" Stanton spat.

Sarah laughed. "Oh, those stereotypes are so two-thousand-twenty," she said with a dismissive wave of her hand. "Black robes? Seriously?"

"Fuck you, Sarah," Stanton spat. "Carlos, please see Ms. Russell out."

Carlos grabbed Sarah's arm. She snatched away from him.

"I'll see myself out, thank you!" she said. "I have to give it to you Patrick, you've got balls. Huge ones! Try not to get them stepped on though, okay, sweetie?"

Sarah turned and walked away.

Stanton turned to Carlos.

"Answer me truthfully," he said. "Are you and your people still on that bitch's payroll?"

"Aren't we all?" Carlos asked.

"You know they'll do to you and your Tigers... excuse me—your CIA Shadow Unit—what they did to the Bloodmen and the other Guilds once they deem you no longer useful."

"I'm way ahead of you," Carlos said. "The situation is being handled as we speak."

"Assassinations?" the president asked.

"No. That would bring on a war we're not ready for yet," Carlos said. "I'm just sending everyone in the Inside a little reminder of how the game is played. What about on your end?"

"Don't worry," the president said. "Prime Minister Butler and the others will play ball. Soon, we won't have to worry about those assholes anymore."

"Good," Carlos said. "No one should have a hold on the President of the United States."

"Come tomorrow, I'll only have you to worry about," Stanton said.

Both men laughed.

CHAPTER SIXTEEN

A modern mansion sat at the feet of Stone Mountain, partially lit by moonlight and a few lights on the estate's grounds. Secret Service Agents patrolled the grounds on foot.

Two black Chrysler 300s pulled up with a black, S-Class Mercedes Benz between them.

Secret Service Agents hopped out of the Chryslers and surrounded the Benz.

Stephen got out of the Benz and the Agents walked him to his door. He went inside.

Someone watched the Agents mill around the mansion through the scope of a rifle.

Atop the roof of a mansion across the road from Stephen's lay Jamela, prone, watching Stephen's home. A black *Howa HCR Rifle* with a Diamond Long Range 4-16x50mm scope sat on a tripod before her.

Jamela peered through the scope and aimed the rifle at Stephen's silhouette in the window of the mansion.

"Stephen, Stephen, Stephen," Jamela whispered. "You're slipping, dude. But, then again, you've never been a target before, have you Stevie?"

Jamela noticed someone crouched down

on the side of the house, sneaking toward one of the Agents. The figure was too far away to make out his face, but to Jamela, something about him was familiar.

"What the hell? Who—?" she said, frowning.

She zoomed the scope in closer to the man's face. She recognized him and she jumped, shaking her head in disbelief.

"Malcolm?" she said, her eyes wide. "Oh, my God, it is Malcolm!"

Jamela spotted an Agent watching Malcolm from the rear of the house.

"Baby, you've been made," she whispered. "Turn around."

The Agent raised his pistol and aimed it at the back of Malcolm's head.

"God damn it, baby! Turn around!" she hissed.

The agent slightly pressed the trigger of his pistol with his index finger.

A moment later, a gunshot thundered across the night sky.

The Agent's head exploded.

Malcolm looked over his shoulder in shock at the headless corpse lying a few yards away from him. He snapped his head up toward the direction of the gunshot that felled the Secret Service Agent. He spotted Jamela and they locked eyes. After a brief while, Malcolm smiled at her warmly. She returned it, tears welling in the corners of her eyes.

A sudden hail of bullets snapped them both out of their stupor.

Bullets chewed the dirt at Malcolm's

feet. He dove to avoid the storm of lead.

Three Agents were hit in the head or neck from bullets raining down on them.

Malcolm stabbed an Agent in the groin with one knife and under the chin with another. The Agent's eyes rolled back in his head.

Another Agent dropped from a bullet that hit him right above his lip and flew out of the center of his back, striking the ground behind him.

The Agents realized where the shots were coming from. A couple of them pointed toward the roof of the mansion across the street and the agents charged toward the building.

Jamela slung the rifle across her back then sprinted toward the side of the house. She rappelled down a rope already hooked to the side of the building and quickly descended to the ground.

Malcolm slit an Agent's throat then hurled his knife into the gut of another Agent a few yards away. The Agent fell onto his back, the knife protruding from the Agent's belly.

Malcolm ran toward the side of the mansion across the street. Jamela ran toward Malcolm. Agents entered the front door of the mansion across the street.

Jamela and Malcolm stopped running a few feet from each other.

Jamela ran to Malcolm, hugged him and wrapped her legs around his waist.

"Baby! You miss me?" she asked.

Malcolm looked over her shoulder. He pointed toward Agents running at them from the back of the mansion.

"Let's hope *they* miss you!"

Jamela released her hold on Malcolm and landed on the ground in front of him.

"Shit!" she shouted. "You lead; I'll follow!"

They sprinted off, just barely evading a storm of bullets.

Malcolm and Jamela ran down the middle of the street.

Suddenly, a black van whipped around the corner and cut them off. The door slid open. Another van screeched to a halt behind Jamela and Malcolm.

The side door of the van in front of them opened. Three men wearing white pants, white hoodies and black ski masks squatted inside the van, staring at Jamela and Malcolm.

Another three hooded men jumped out of the van behind them, firing tranquilizer darts into Malcolm's and Jamela's backs.

Jamela staggered against Malcolm and Malcolm almost fell. Both of them were dazed and unsteady.

Two of the men jumped out of the van in front of them then threw pillowcases over the couple's heads and tossed the dazed Bloodmen into the open van. Both vans sped off into the crisp Atlanta night.

To Be Continued in "Ngolo: Vendetta"

NGOLO ORIGINS

KAMARA

His name was Kamara Keita and he was the Master of Ngolo.

His ancestors created the martial art called *Ngolo* long before they migrated from the forests of Gabon to the rolling, sandy plains of Senegal. He learned as a boy that his Grand Ancestor, Ngaa Mfumu, traveled throughout what is today known as Gabon and the Congo, asking women how they would escape this hold, block this sword strike, or execute this throw. In his wisdom, he believed that while men relied on strength, speed and ferocity in combat, women relied on masterful technique—a two hundred pound man would fight much differently than a hundred pound woman—and that a man could now add his strength, speed and ferocity to the technical genius of women and become the most formidable of warriors. And he was right.

Ngaa Mfumu began to train his family in his fighting system, which he named Ngolo—*power.*

A thousand years later, Kamara's mother, the Nfumu'loo—*Grandmaster*—of Ngolo began offering her services as a protection specialist to the wealthy and powerful business people, Imams and Sheiks in Senegal and the young Kamara would tag along on these assignments and eventually assist his mother in her protection details.

When he was sixteen, young Kamara travelled to the United States for the first time to enroll in Howard University, where he remained until his second year of medical school, when his mother fell ill and, as her only child, he had to return to Senegal to take over the family's protection business.

But after a while, no contracts came. Former clients preferred paying the less expensive off-duty police officers and thugs in suits that paying top dollar for the best security money could buy.

All those who had come to the House of Keita and their Ngolo were no more.

To make matters worse, most of Kamara's young cousins were not interested in learning Ngolo, and those who were did not have the discipline to keep the system alive.

And so, Kamara shut down the family's business and prepared to return to medical school. And then they came.

A young Black man came to Kamara's door and, looking inside, saw nothing, except complete darkness.

"Hello," the man said in English. Then in Mandinka, "Abenyadi." Then, when he received no response, he said in French, "Umm... bonjour?"

"Try Wolof," Kamara's voice came from the dark.

"Salaamaalikum!"

"I knew you'd use that colonizer's tongue," Kamara said. "I said Wolof, not Arabic."

"But you're speaking to me in English, now," the man said.

"Wolof!"

"Oh, okay," the man said. "Umm... na nga def?"

"Very good," Kamara whispered. "Mangi fi rekk. Na nga def?"

"Jaam rek."

"Who are you?" Kamara's voice now came from behind the man.

The man whirled about, his eyes wide. "My name is Antonio Jones, Guild Professor of the Bloodmen."

"Bloodmen?"

"Yes. Assassinations are now legal worldwide as long as they are sanctioned by one of the world governments that is part of the International Alliance, as I'm sure you well know."

"No."

"Well, we Bloodmen are the first guild of assassins to receive a charter. Our roster includes Black men from throughout the Diaspora that are former special operators for various militaries around the globe, former CIA and MI-6 black ops and former Nigerian Defense Intelligence Agency special agents."

"Okay."

"We seek your services. We want you to train us. May I come in?"

"Yes."

They walk into Kamara's house. Kamara claps his hands and the lights in the house come on, illuminating a living room with an oxblood leather couch and matching loveseat and chair. Kamara sat in the chair. Jones sat opposite him on the couch.

Kamara picked up a slim controller from the coffee table and turned off the fifty-inch television screen on the wall.

"Would you like some tea?" Kamara asked. Wait, you're American. Coffee?"

"No, sir. So, what do you think of my proposition?"

"I've never killed anyone in my life," Kamara said. "I protect, not kill."

"Would you have killed to protect one of your clients?"

"I'm good enough at my job that I never had to."

"You'll be paid a shitload of money," Jones said.

"I don't need loads of shit."

"What do you need?"

"Nothing from you," Kamara said. "What martial arts do you Bloodmen study now?"

"We're trying to stay true to our Diasporan culture and theme," Jones said. "So, we're studying 52 Blocks, Esgrima Con Machete and Capoeira Angola. Mixing it with military tactics and techniques."

"All good systems," Kamara said. "But Ngolo will take those systems beyond what you can fathom."

"So that's a yes?"

"As long as Ngolo is all the Bloodmen

study."

"And the military ops, of course," Jones said.

"No," Kamara said. "Ngolo only; or nothing."

"But the firearms... the driving," Jones said.

"All part of Ngolo," Kamara said. "You think the Keita family has spent the last thousand years protecting towns, villages, politicians, religious figures and celebrities with kicks and punches?"

"Well, I thought..."

"Just Ngolo," Kamara said.

"Well, my father told me to give you whatever you want, so just Ngolo."

"And who is your father?"

"Guildmaster Stokely Jones," Jones replied. "Founder of the Bloodmen."

"And he is a Pisces."

"What? How did you know?"

"Ngolo."

"Damn! Your martial training includes how to read minds."

"Hell no," Kamara said. "It includes how to find shit on Google really fast."

Kamara held up a cell phone with Stokely Jones' photo on the screen.

Kamara rose. "I'll pack my things."

JAMELA

Part One

Bob Marley's *Crazy Baldheads* wafted from the speakers hanging from the exposed concrete ceiling. Raising a mug of chai latte to her lips, Jamela slowly peered across the room, settling her gaze on a portly man with ruddy skin and combed over blond hair that would make any 45th president envious. He wore a charcoal gray tracksuit, with a white t-shirt underneath, and gray running shoes. His eyes widened as he nervously checked his phone; again.

Jamela set her mug down and stared at the tarot card laid out before her on the table. The young woman sitting across from her looked down at the cards, her huge afro casting a shadow over them. The woman looks up at Jamela.

"The Magician card in reverse warns you to watch out for trickery, manipulation, or betrayal," the card reader said. "Next, we have the Hierophant, which represents rules, regulations, and traditions. The Hierophant next to the reversed Magician means that you are part of some tradition or traditional organization that is good for you and has taught you a lot, but within that group is a traitor, your enemy."

"Hmm," Jamela said, twirling one of her locs with her index finger.

The portly man stood and stretched his neck, dipping his head from side-to-side.

Jamela reached into the breast pocket of her red and black plaid shirt and pulled out a fat wad of money. She peeled off a hundred-dollar bill and placed it on top of the cards.

"Thanks, Shaniqua."

Shaniqua picked up the money and stuffed it into her bra. "But your reading isn't finished."

"No need," Jamela said. "Traitor in my organization is a lot to unpack. Thanks, again!"

The pudgy man looked at his phone once more, then brought his hand up to wipe the nervous sweat from his face. His eyes nervously darted around the coffee house.

Jamela walked toward the counter and pretended to look at the menu of teas, coffees and vegan sandwiches written in chalk on a board mounted on the wall behind the cashier.

The pudgy man sprang from his seat and headed for the door.

Jamela change courses and nonchalantly left the coffee house.

Jamela paused to take out her cell phone and double-check her assignment.

"Yep, that's him," she whispered.

Winston Bailey, lawyer for *Adelphon En-*

tertainment Industries. He had stolen and leaked the screenplays to four of *Webflix*'s upcoming big budget movies when Webflix refused to merge with Adelphon. The dirty move had cost Webflix half a billion dollars, so they had enlisted the services of the Bloodmen to take Bailey off the board.

This was Jamela's first mark without a partner and she wanted to make a good impression. As the first woman in the Bloodmen to receive a solo contract, she was determined to pave the way for other sisters in the greatest Guild on the planet.

Jamela carefully increased her pace as she mentally took stock of her weapons—her pair of eagle talon-like karambits on her belt near the small of her back; the folding knives in each pocket; and the compact Sig Sauer P320 .357 pistol in a holster sewn inside her leather jacket.

Jamela paused as Winston glanced over his shoulder, a leer on his face as he caught her looking.

"Hey, Soul Sister," he said, waggling his eyebrows.

Ew.

Then an idea came to her: she would make Winston's fetish for a sister work in her favor. Reaching up, Jamela ran her fingers through her soft locs and smiled. She then pulled her cell phone out of her pocket and pressed it to her ear, pretending to talk on it as she continued to walk behind Winston down the street.

Putting an extra sway in her hips, Jamela pretended to be too absorbed in her phone conversation to notice Winston stop and step off to the side, watching her with his shifty eyes.

As Jamela came even with where he was standing, she forced herself to remain loose and relaxed. Winston stepped out in front of her, the swift movement causing Jamela to bump into his sour sweaty body. Jamela must have been taller than he realized, surprise flashed across his face as they came almost eye to eye. Snatching her phone from her hand, he gestured lewdly to her chest, as his other hand grabbed a fistful of her hair and yanked her head back painfully.

"A little flatter than I like, but you'll do," Winston snickered. "I'm gonna have fun with you before you tell me who sent you and why. What, to get photos of me in some compromising position? We're gonna get into all kinds of positions."

Jamela drew the karambits from her belt then punched both sides of Winston's neck, driving the hooked knives deep into his carotid arteries. She yanked the knives out of the lawyer's neck, flicked his blood from the knives onto the pavement then slid the karambits back into their sheaths.

A fountain of blood arced from both sides of his neck. Winston's eyes rolled up into his head and then he fell with a thud.

A Dodge charger pulled up to the sidewalk near Jamela with a screech. A strobe light inside its grill flashed.

Jamela took her authorization papers

out of her pocket and held them before her.

"This is a legitimate contract. I'm a Bloodman."

An elder woman steps out of the car smoking a big cigar.

Jamela smiles.

"Manman Cécile," Jamela said. "The only pig I mess with."

Manman Cécile was in her 60s, but still attractive, with silver goddess braids that lay on her shoulders, and an athletic build.

"Not too many cops are Vodouisant," Manman Cécile said. "And even less are Mambo or Houngan."

She waves her hand dismissively then looks around.

"You can put those papers away. We're good. Where's Malcolm?"

"I'm working solo."

Manman Cécile looks surprised. "What? They finally let you work ninety-nine, huh?"

"Yep."

"Good. If anybody's ready, you are, Marinette."

"I've been meaning to ask, why do you always call me Marinette?"

"Marinette Bwa Chech is one of the fiercest of the Lwa," the detective replied. "She is the revolution. She is bloodshed, violence and fire. When I see you, I see her."

"I'm flattered."

Tilting her head with a slightly unnatural movement, Manman Cécile gazed at the man on the ground, her brown eyes taking in the dual slits in the sides of Winston's neck.

Her eyes traveled along the blood spray and up to Jamela, a slight smirk on her face.

"Okay, I see you, sis."

Jamela smiled.

"Okay, I've gotta get to the Ile and give a report to Papa," Jamela said. "You be safe out here."

"You be safe, Bloodman... err, woman," Manman Cécile said. "Y'all really should re-think that name."

"Been the 'Bloodmen' since before anyone alive today even knew we existed," Jamela said with a shrug. "Before the world came to its senses and made sanctioned assassinations legal. I doubt that's changing anytime soon."

"I hear that," Manman Cécile said. "Choose your battles wisely and shit. Take care, sis. Let me get the Medical Examiner over here."

"All right, Detective. Buh-bye."

Jamela jogged across the street to her candy apple red Ducati Scrambler motorcycle, hopped on and sped off.

* * *

Walking into the receiving room of the Bloodmen's Ile, Jamela was relieved to see it mostly deserted and quickly made her way toward the women's locker room.

Making her way to her usual locker, Jamela locked her weapons and clothing inside

She walks toward the showers, pausing

to look at herself in the full-length mirror on the wall just beyond the row of sinks. Her body was mostly lean muscle and well-toned. She flexed the muscles in her bicep like a posing bodybuilder and laughed then stepped into the steaming hot shower.

Part Two

Jamela cruised up a driveway riddled by crunchy brown leaves. She stopped at the end of it, a few feet from the steps that led up to the rectangular two-flat's front porch. She hopped off the motorcycle and jogged up the stairs then pressed her palm to a panel beside the opaque glass front door. The door opened a crack.

The sound of hip-hop music met her ears. Jamela drew her karambits then slid along the wall, knives poised and ready.

Then she heard, "Bim! Bim! Bim!" come from her living room.

Jamela rolled her eyes then sheathed her karambits.

"Morocco! What the hell are you doing here?"

Rounding the corner, Jamela bit back a stream of obscenities. A lanky teenager was sprawled along her couch, his giant shoes carelessly leaving traces of dirt where his feet precariously dangled over her end table. He sat up, his wild afro bouncing, and flashed a wide smile. He pressed the remote control and the music video on the wide television screen on the wall went silent.

"Mela, hope you don't mind, I needed to get out of the house and figured I'd crash here for a few hours."

Swatting at his monstrous feet until he groaned and finally moved so Jamela had room to sit, Jamela reached over and snagged the bag of barbecue chips off his chest.

"I gave you and Head keys to feed and walk Petey Wheatstraw when I'm out of town and to come here in case of an emergency. Why did you have to get out of the house? Was there an emergency? Where's Head?"

Snatching the bag back from Jamela and holding it just out of reach, Morocco smirked.

"What's with the twenty questions? Aren't you happy to see your favorite mentee?"

Rolling her eyes pointedly at his dirty shoes, her half-eaten bag of chips and the crumbs scattered around him, Jamela blew out a long-suffering sigh.

"Maybe I should have looked the other way when those *Bring Back the Old South* college boys were gonna string up you and Head for defacing their bus. My life would be so much simpler."

"That's cold, Jamela," Morocco said. "You know we were striking a blow against white supremacy."

"I don't know how revolutionary it is to paint a thousand tiny white penises all over the bus, but okay."

"But you gotta admit that shit was funny, though."

He extended his fist toward Jamela. Jamela gave him a pound.

"It was aight," she muttered.

Morocco brushed the rest of the offending crumbs off his shirt and onto Jamela's floor.

"And Head is exactly why I'm here. Bruh finally got himself a date and you know his mama ain't letting him bring a girl to her holy home, so he's using my crib. My folks are at the coffee house... which my Daddy called and said a hit took place in front of just a little while ago. Know anything about that?"

He looked at her suspiciously.

"Never mind all that," Jamela said, waving her hand dismissively. "Why is Head taking a girl on a date to your house, not to a restaurant, or the movies, or the doggone High Museum, or something?"

"Come on, Jamela. Really?"

Jamela shook her head. "Nasty asses. I hope he's got protection."

I hooked him up with a couple before I left."

"Who is this poor girl? Jamela asked.

"I don't know much about her," Morocco replied. "But her name is Lewa. She's a Freshman at Spelman, so she must be smart since she's our age."

Jamela walked over to the small kitchen then opened the stainless-steel refrigerator. She reached in and grabbed a beer.

Morocco craned his neck to see what Jamela was doing.

"Hey, toss me one of those," he said

Jamela tossed a cream soda over her shoulder at Morocco. Smiling, Morocco caught the bottle. He looked at its label and his smile faded. He shrugged, removed the top with the bottle opener on the table and began to guzzle the soda.

Jamela sat back down next to Morocco. "What does this Elewa look like?"

"She's foine," Morocco said, pursing his lips. "Curly faux-hawk; skin almost as black as her hair; big old booty!"

Jamela rolled her eyes.

"I won't lie, she's a little scary, though." He said.

"Scary?"

Morocco took another swig of cream soda. "I'm just saying, for a seventeen-year-old, she looks like she's seen some things. Know what I mean?"

"I think so."

Morocco smiled. "So, what's up with you and old boy? Malcolm?"

"He was my Field Trainer. He's cool."

"I bet he's training you, all right."

Frowning, Jamela pointed at Morocco. "Naw, it's not like that. Date the son of my Guildmaster? Naw."

"You think he's fine, though," Morocco said, giving Jamela the side-eye.

"He *is* fine. And smart. And funny. And respectful."

"Shoot your shot, then."

"I don't know."

"Look, Jamela. You're pretty, tough, really physically fit, funny and smart yourself.

He'd be lucky to have you."

Jamela stares at Morocco. "Damn. When did you get so mature?"

Morocco blushes. "You think I'm mature? Then maybe you and I could—"

Jamela rolls her eyes. "Here we go."

Morocco laughs.

Jamela looks around, swiveling her head from side to side. "Morocco, where's Petey Wheatstraw?"

"Oh, he wanted to go out for a few minutes before you got home," Morocco said. He's out back."

Panic shot through Jamela. "You let a hundred- and fifty-pound Rottweiler just run outside unsupervised and without a leash?"

"Petey ain't gonna hurt nobody," Morocco said.

"He's was literally raised by the Benetti family to kill people," Jamela said. "I've just been retraining him since I took the Benetti's out."

Spinning toward the door, Jamela slammed her beer down and threw the door open.

"Petey Wheatstraw, come here boy! Petey Wheatstraw!"

Arm thrown over the back of the couch, Morocco watched Jamela curiously. "What's the big deal? He's a good dog. He'll be back after he plays for a little bit. We do this all the time when you're out of town."

"Dammit, Morocco! I'm a Bloodman. Any kills associated with me that aren't sanctioned by the Guild and I'm dead!"

A deep bark and a man's laughter drew Jamela's attention across the street. Her hand clutched her chest in shock as she watched her big dog happily bound after the tennis ball her neighbor threw.

"Petey Wheatstraw?" Jamela called out.

Petey Wheatstraw ignored her. His playmate, on the other hand, did not. With a wide smile on his face, the man wiped his hands off on his jeans as he jogged over to her, dirt-smudged across a very expensive-looking dress shirt. The knot of his green and gold paisley silk tie was pulled loose and flopped in time with his steps.

"Hello, I'm guessing this big guy is yours? I'm Mofetolu, but call me Tolu, for short. I live right over there. I hope you don't mind, I figured I'd try to distract him a little to make sure he didn't run away."

Mofetolu stuck his hand out as he spoke, his brown eyes friendly and his smile genuine.

"Oh, hello, I'm Jamela, and yeah, he's mine. Sorry, I've never seen him so friendly with someone he doesn't know before."

Grasping Mofetolu's hand firmly, Jamela watched Petey Wheatstraw as he trotted over to them, tail wagging. Tolu reached down and scratched Petey Wheatstraw on the head, the dog's black ears swiveled toward Jamela as he dropped the ball, tongue lolling out of his mouth.

Chuckling, Tolu stepped back from Jamela. "I've always gotten along well with animals. I haven't had a dog since I moved here from Lagos."

"Petey, you know you aren't supposed to wander off." Jamela said wagging a finger at her dog.

Sitting down, Petey Wheatstraw tilted his enormous head at Jamela.

"Don't look at me like that," Jamela said, glaring at Petey Wheatstraw.

Tolu laughed as he bent over and picked up the ball, lightly tossing it up as he stood.

"Well, I'm glad Petey Wheatstraw ventured across the street today. It gave me a chance to play with a dog and of course to meet you. Do you have an email address or number you'd like to share in case he gets out again? That way I can contact you?"

"Oh, sure! I mean, it's unlikely he'd ever get loose again, but um, yeah."

Fumbling in her pocket to retrieve her phone, a snicker coming from behind Jamela drew her attention. Morocco stood nonchalantly leaning on her door, sipping his cream soda while watching them.

"Oh! I didn't realize you have a boyfriend! I'm so sorry if I was being too forward asking for your number."

"W'sup, player?" Morocco said stone-faced.

Tolu shifted uncomfortably.

Jamela jerked a thumb in Morocco's direction. "Morocco is definitely not my boyfriend! You think I'm out here robbing cradles and shit? He's my friend and he's only seventeen!"

Morocco frowned. "Only."

"Give me a second Tolu," Jamela said, unlocking her cell phone. "If you give me your number, I'll put you in my phone and then call you, that way you'll have my number."

Tolu pulled out his own phone, a confident smile growing on his face.

Petey Wheatstraw gave a little yip and laid down.

Jamela leaned over and ruffled the hair between the dog's ears. Petey Wheatstraw smiled and let his tongue loll out happily.

Tolu gave Jamela his number. As Jamela turned, snapping her fingers for Petey Wheatstraw to follow, which he did, Tolu called out for Jamela to wait a second.

"I don't know what your schedule looks like tomorrow," he said. "But I was thinking of trying out that new ice cream place that opened up about a five-minute walk from here. Would you and Petey Wheatstraw like to try it out tomorrow night?"

"Oh, um—" Jamela stuttered in surprise. Petey Wheatstraw bumped her leg in encouragement.

"Yeah, that sounds fun. After dinner? Why don't you send me a text and let me know what time?"

"Great! I'll see you two tomorrow!" Tolu started walking toward his house.

"Hey Tolu!"

Tolu turned back around with a curious look on his face.

"My name is Jamela, but all my friends call me Mela."

Smiling Tolu waved goodbye, "See you

tomorrow, Mela!"

Smiling, Jamela walked inside the house, Petey Wheatstraw by her side.

* * *

Sunlight shined in through her bedroom window and warmed Jamela's face. Yawning and stretching, Jamela tossed one leg out of the bed. Her phone beeped. With a sigh, Jamela glanced at the screen, a message from Morocco popped up:

C u at the party Friday. The dashiki you got me is fye! Thank u!

"Please, Ogun. Don't let Head and Morocco embarrass me at the keta."

Jamela grumbled and kicked off her covers. She threw her other leg out of bed and headed to the kitchen to feed Petey Wheatstraw and check his water. He padded out from the guest bedroom, yawning and showing all of his sharp white teeth.

"Petey, I'm going to the park for a run this morning. You interested? If so, I'll take the car instead of the bike."

Petey Wheatstraw looked up from his bowl and fixed his eyes on Jamela a moment before licking his lips and going back to his food.

"I take that as a yes," Jamela said.

She headed into the bathroom in her bedroom to brush her teeth and throw on some workout clothes.

Fifteen minutes later, water bottle and leash in hand, Jamela jingled her car keys. "Alright Petey, let's go! See if you can keep up with me old man!"

Jamela slipped a folding knife into her long sleeve rash guard, clipping it onto the strap of her sports bra.

Petey Wheatstraw trotted up to the door and shook his fur. Jamela reached down and placed his leather collar on.

* * *

Jamela pulled her candy apple red Corvette into a space in the park's lot. She hopped out of the car and Petey Wheatstraw followed.

The sun was out, providing some comforting warmth to the cool fall morning. Jamela set out on the jogging path, Petey Wheatstraw trotting alongside her.

About a mile into her run, Jamela was starting to work up a good sweat. Raised voices broke through the secluded patch Jamela was running through, and suddenly she found herself coming upon a very large group of people. Jamela began to slow down; she was more than a little shocked when she quickly realizing this wasn't a typical large gathering. This was a gathering of three dozen white hipsters with five Black women three Black men and a Black teenage boy and girl encircled by them.

The hipsters all wore blue polo shirts with white piping on their collars and blue denim hoodies over them. They also wore navy blue joggers and white skate shoes.

"Bring Back the Old South," Jamela whispered. "Out here?"

Bring Back the Old South was a far-right neo-fascist organization that promoted Southern white pride and political violence. The group sees white men people and Western culture worldwide as under siege.

Angry shouts and startled yells pulled Jamela's attention to the far side of the crowd. Right out in the open stood Spencer Duke, the eldest son of Rufus Duke, the extremely dangerous and charismatic leader of Bring Back the Old South.

A loud boom sounded and everything began to go sideways.

The sounds of gunfire rang out in the park, followed by terrified screams and shouts.

Chaos exploded.

Jamela sprinted toward the mob. She watched as the crowd turned feral and began brutally attacking the Black men, women and teens trapped by them.

"Leave it to me to jog right into the middle of a lynching," Jamela said.

She darted around a tree and ran full force into a white man who was beating the teenage boy into a bloody pulp.

Tossing the gasping teen onto the ground, the man grinned a crooked toothy smile at Jamela, cracking his knuckles sinisterly as he stomped toward her.

Jamela ran straight at him.

The man swung a wide hook punch at

Jamela's face.

Jamela dropped to the ground, sliding on her knees just below his reach.

She drew the folding knife from her bra and slammed it down into the man's combat boot.

The man screamed as he dropped to one knee.

Jamela yanked the knife out of his foot then sliced the back of his leg just above his ankle, severing his Achilles tendon.

The man fell onto his side, wailing in agony.

Hearing another scream, Jamela whirled around to see Spencer Duke strangling one of the Black women. The woman's feet dangled as she fought to stay conscious.

A deep bark got Jamela's attention. She looked down at Petey Wheatstraw, who now stood at her side.

Reaching down, Jamela clumsily unhooked the dog's collar. Growling, the Rottweiler raced ahead of Jamela.

"Let her go, Spencer!" Jamela screamed as she ran toward the heavily muscled blond behemoth.

Spencer gave his choking victim a hard shake then tossed her unconscious body aside. His cold blue eyes met Jamela's.

Petey Wheatstraw leapt at Spencer.

Spencer drew a matte black Smith and Wesson *Judge* revolver from his jacket and fired. The sound of thunder rent the morning sky as a .410 shotgun shell exploded out of the revolver's muzzle.

Petey fell to the ground with a thud, whimpering as blood pumped from the huge wound in his chest.

"No!" Jamela screamed.

Spencer aimed the revolver at Jamela's face.

Jamela hurled her knife toward Spencer then rolled for cover behind a big oak tree.

Spencer fired. Dirt and grass flew up in the air less than an inch behind her.

Spencer screamed and began firing madly.

Jamela peeked from behind the tree and saw Spencer firing blindly, her knife jutting from the socket of his right eye.

After a few moments, Spencer fell onto his back. He convulsed once then lay still.

Jamela ran to Petey Wheatstraw, dropped to her knees beside the dog and wrapped her arms around his big body. Sobbing into his fur, Jamela laid in the grass beside her friend.

Part Three

Irkutsk, Russia.

A gust of wind blew a sheet of hissing ice crystals around Jamela's *Mountain 600 Danner* boots. She wrapped her arms tightly around herself and pulled the zipper of her winter jacket up higher on her neck.

A fresh gust of wind pushed her sideways.

"Goddamn Irkutsk," she whispered. "This is what I get for helping my people against crazy ass white supremacists in a world run by crazy ass white supremacists."

"This is what you get for almost killing Spencer Duke," said a voice that came from her ear buds. "If you had killed him, things would be worse. We don't do unsanctioned hits."

"Yeah, yeah, Malcolm," Jamela said. "What about that guy in Japan? My would-be rapist?"

"I don't know what the hell you're talking about... on this line that could be monitored."

"Copy that."

She raised a pair of digital binoculars to her face. A figure walked out of the side door of a three-story building and trudged toward an SUV waiting several yards away.

"Hold up. The mark has left the building," Jamela said. "I'm gonna do him here."

"No," Malcolm said. "Follow him to his house and close the contract there."

"It's too cold here," Jamela said, tossing her binoculars into a backpack that sat in the snow next to a white M40A5 long-range rifle. "I'm gonna end him so I can get to my next sucky job."

"Jamela!"

"Talk to you later, Malcolm."

"Jamela, don't fuck this—"

Jamela removed her ear buds and slipped them into the pocket in her sleeve.

She picked up the rifle and placed its tripod a foot in front of her. She scooted toward the rifles scope and peered into it. The mark was a foot from the front of his SUV.

Jamela inhaled deeply then held her breath. She squeezed the trigger slowly then fired.

The mark fell against the hood of his vehicle then slid down to the snow-covered ground.

Jamela put her ear buds back in.

"The job's done," she whispered.

"Jamela, you're crazier than a shoeshine in a shit storm," Malcolm said. "Your next job is with me. I've gotta keep tabs on you."

"Not back to partner gigs," Jamela said, frowning.

"It's in Hawaii," Malcolm said. "Or you can take that solo gig in Ahvaz, Iran. I hear it's a balmy 129 degrees this time of year."

"Hawaii it is," Jamela said.

"Thought so."

"Bring your swimming trunks," Jamela said. "And boxer briefs. I like blue."

"What?" Malcolm said.

"I'm shooting my shot."

"Oh," Malcolm said.

"Did it work?"

"We'll see when we meet in Hawaii," Malcolm said. "Peace."

"Peace."

Jamela smiled as she broke down her rifle and slipped its pieces into her backpack.

"Morocco would be proud," she said.

She stood and walked down the quiet street, strong winds pushing her forward and forcing her to jog. But her mind wasn't on the freezing cold and snow. It was on Malcolm, and Morocco and Petey Wheatstraw and how she would one day be the best assassin the Bloodmen had ever produced and earn the code name of *Marinette*.

MALCOLM AND JAMELA

MALCOLM's black *Lamborghini Urus* SUV sped through alleys and down quiet, early morning streets.

His fellow Bloodman, J-Boogie—a mountain of a man that called Detroit home—rode shotgun, blowing the smoke from his fat Cuban cigar out of the SUV's rolled down window.

In the back seat sat Jamela, the best assassin in the Bloodmen after the guild's Professor, Stephen, Malcolm and Guildmaster Kamara himself. She was also the craziest, according to Malcolm. But he loved her anyway.

They'd headed southeast and, after confirming there was no surveillance behind, Malcolm circled around and headed northwest. Gradually, the darkness of the early morning dissipated and the Daba Mountains appeared, looming in the distance. Malcolm stopped in Ciqikou, a 1000-year-old town in the Shapingba District of Chongqing, China. Throngs of men, women and children walked Ciqikou's steep and narrow pedestrian streets. Even though it was early, shops were open and selling their wares—porcelain, other handicrafts, and gifts—while restaurants and tea houses gave visitors a taste of ancient Chinese cuisine.

Foregoing the tactical field uniform of the Bloodmen, Malcolm and J-Boogie wore skinny jeans, a Henley shirt and a blazer. Malcolm's blazer was brown corduroy and J-Boogie's was blue wool. Underneath their blazers they carried 9mm pistols and spare ammunition. Jamela wore a yellow pants suit and white blouse. She also carried a pistol with extra ammunition.

Malcolm, J-Boogie, and Jamela stepped out of the SUV and strolled down a street of shops. Red oval and onion-shaped paper lamps hung down from the rafters in front of every store.

The trio walked through the myriad of shops, which provided multiple venues for Malcolm, J-Boogie, and Jamela to exit and enter.

After completing their surveillance detection walk, they boarded a second SUV—a silver *Great Wall Haval H6*—then sped off.

After a short while of driving toward the mountain, the SUV came to a halt, and Malcolm, J-Boogie, and Jamela departed the vehicle. Malcolm, J-Boogie and Jamela strolled through the busy streets, scanning the area for threats.

"You know, we should really have more firepower for this," J-Boogie said.

"That's why I picked you and Malcolm," Jamela said.

"Your asset is coming alone, right?" J-Boogie asked.

"That's the plan," she said calmly.

"But he could show up with others," J-Boogie said.

Jamela walked as if she didn't have a care in the world. "Anything is possible."

J-Boogie shook his head. "We should have more firepower."

They passed an elderly street vendor selling dumplings and various flavors of bubble tea from a cart under a huge umbrella. Jamela and her partners cut across the street to a restaurant called Nanluoguxiang.

Inside, they tried to appear nonchalant while observing the customers for signs of danger. There were only a handful of diners in the place and half of the tables remained empty.

"Did you charge the masks fully before we left the hotel?" J-Boogie whispered. "Three Black folks would stand out like a sore thumb in here."

"In here?" Malcolm said. "In all of Ciqikou."

"Y'all trippin', acting like this is my first protection gig."

"It is," Malcolm said. "That's why you asked us to help."

"Well, it's not my first gig," Jamela said, raising her index finger skyward. "I don't know why somebody would hire a guild of assassins to protect them, anyway."

Because we're experts at protecting ourselves and each other out here, so they figure we can do the same for them."

"I guess I can for what we're being paid," Jamela said.

"I heard that," Malcolm said.

"So, did you charge the masks?" J-Boogie asked, frowning.

"Yeah, J-Boog," Jamela said. "Chill. To these folks, you'll look like a bigger version of Ludi Lin or some shit until our asset is safe and we're on the way home."

They sat in a booth away from the windows. The waiter arrived, and Malcolm, speaking fluent Mandarin, ordered drinks while they "waited for a friend."

J-Boogie looked at Jamela and quietly asked, "How sure are you that Jianlian is gonnao show?"

"Fifty-fifty," she said.

J-Boogie gave Malcolm a look of concern.

"That's what she always says," Malcolm said. "The assets gonna show."

"Debrief us again," J-Boogie said.

Jamela rolled her eyes and sighed.

"Like I said before," Jamela began. "Jianlian, former COO, had a falling out with the CEO of Yibin Insurance after announcing he was leaving Yibin and was going to start his own insurance firm. They killed his wife and child to punish him. He knows he's next."

"Why didn't he hire Hung Gerk Kune to protect him?" J-Boogie asked.

"Because Yibin had already hired them to kill him." Jamela replied.

They drank and talked quietly for about an hour, then a man with a mustache and goatee wearing a blue hoodie, baggy jeans and blue skate shoes walked into the restaurant, fidgeting as he glanced nervously around.

"That's him," Jamela said.

Jamela locked eyes with the man and nodded slightly.

Jianlian rushed toward her table, almost bumping into a waiter. He sat at the booth beside J-Boogie.

"You ready to go?" Jamela asked.

"I don't know," Jianlian said.

The waiter interrupted, handing them menus, then left to give them a moment to decide.

Jianlian's eyes darted around the restaurant before he gave his menu to Jamela. "Not hungry."

When the waiter returned, they all ordered in Mandarin and the waiter left to take their orders to the kitchen.

Jamela leaned over the table and spoke quietly to Jianlian, "We can protect you. You can live in the US like we talked about."

"You don't know Yibin," Jianlian said. "They will find me."

"They won't find you," Jamela said. "I'll make sure."

"How can you make sure?"

Two stern-eyed burly men walked into the restaurant and studied the interior.

Malcolm discreetly unstrapped his holster and drew his pistol. He held it on his lap under the table. J-Boogie's slight movements indicated that he was doing the same.

Crack! Jianlian's drinking glass erupted. One of the restaurant windows had shattered.

Malcolm crouched and brought his weapon up to search for targets. Jianlian fell out of his chair, and Jamela pulled him away from the line of fire. J-Boogie flipped over the table with a loud thud, creating a shield for them. One waiter froze and the other dove to the deck as two customers dashed for the side door.

The stern-eyed burly pair seemed to have spotted Jianlian, and they opened their leather dusters, exposing *QBZ-95* automatic bullpup-style rifles, and then raised them in Jianlian's direction.

Using an upturned table for cover, Malcolm shot the quickest-moving burly man twice in the chest before shifting to his slower partner and shooting him once in the chest.

Malcolm adjusted his position for a clearer line of sight and aimed at the slower man's face. He squeezed the trigger.

The man's head snapped back and he fell, unmoving.

With the same efficiency, Malcolm dispatched the other man.

J-Boogie fired in the direction of the shattered window.

Jamela and Jianlian crawled away, toward the kitchen, following the retreat of waiters. The remaining customers fled the restaurant through the side door.

Outside, more men with QBZs descended on the restaurant. Their muzzles flashed. Inside, windows imploded, and a salvo of projectiles ripped into Malcolm and J-Boogie's table. The wood wouldn't hold much longer before the bullets broke through.

Malcolm and J-Boogie scrambled to another table, and Malcolm flipped it to its side. He and J-Boogie used it as a shield while they fired in the direction of the muzzle flashes. Malcolm's gun ran empty, and with a fluid motion, one hand ejected the empty magazine while the other brought up a fresh one. He inserted the full magazine and depressed the slide stop release. The slide sprang forward and a new bullet loaded into the chamber.

Jamela and Jianlian had disappeared into the kitchen. Malcolm and J-Boogie turned toward the kitchen to make their escape.

A loud *woosh* sounded behind them—the distinctive sound of a rocket-propelled grenade. The RPG exploded. Its concussion caused Malcolm to stumble. On either side of Malcolm and J-Boogie, chairs and tables scattered as if thrown by a typhoon, but the Bloodmen remained on their feet.

They scrambled into the kitchen and joined Jamela. Jianlian was under a nearby table, shaken, but he seemed unharmed. Waiters and kitchen staff were hunkered down for safety. Malcolm squatted as he threw open the back door and aimed his weapon outside. Bullets snapped the air where he would've been standing, and he spotted ruptures of light in the direction from where the shots had come. Instinctively, he fired at the flickers, and the outline of a man dropped. Malcolm glanced down the opposite way of the shady alley where a frightened woman froze in fear. "Clear!"

He glanced behind to find Jamela and Jianlian following while J-Boogie brought up rear security. Malcolm slipped into the alley and headed in the direction of their vehicle. Gunshots sounded behind them, the smaller caliber of J-Boogie's pistol, but Malcolm had his responsibility in front and couldn't neglect it. He trusted J-Boogie to cover their six.

Malcolm made his way around the block to the car and jumped in the driver's seat. J-Boogie swung open the back door and covered Jamela and Jian as they piled in the back. J-Boogie slammed the SUV's door then took his seat up front beside Malcolm.

Malcolm burned rubber, observing everything in front while J-Boogie kept a lookout behind.

"Anyone wounded?" Malcolm asked.

"Jianlian and I are okay," Jamela said.

When J-Boogie didn't reply, Malcolm took his eyes off the road ahead of them and looked over at his friend. "Boog, you okay?"

J-Boogie faced the window, but he wasn't moving.

"Boog?" Malcolm asked.

"Did you see that RPG explode right around us?" J-Boogie asked. "Shit exploded on both sides of us, but *we* didn't explode."

"We got lucky," Malcolm said.

"Naw, that wasn't luck," J-Boogie said.

"We've always been lucky," Malcolm said.

"That was a miracle." J-Boogie said.

"You don't believe in miracles," Malcolm chuckled.

"I do now," J-Boogie said. "Don't they have miracles in your Ifa... and your Vodou, Jamela?"

"Yeah, I guess," Malcolm said. "But—"

"Shit blew up on both sides of us, but we didn't blow up," J-Boogie said. "Doesn't that qualify?"

"Shit happens," Malcolm replied.

"That wasn't like ordinary 'shit happens' kind of shit. That was more like the ancestors protecting us kind of shit."

"Okay, if you say so, it was a miracle." Malcolm said.

"I say so," J-Boogie said decisively.

They rode south and switched vehicles in a small town before heading to the airport.

"Hey Jamela," J-Boogie said.

"What's up?" Jamela responded.

"Tell me about Mama Cécile and Haitian Vodou."

Malcolm shook his head and sped up the road.

STEPHEN

"How about Park Ranger?"

Stephen knew it was coming. His Uncle Marco was a special agent with the elite Investigative Services Branch of the National Park Service, homegrown equivalent to the FBI, charged with investigating the most complex crimes committed on the more than 85 million acres of national parks, monuments, historical sites, and preserves administered by the National Park Service, from Alaska's Noatak National Preserve to Hawaii's Volcanoes National Park.

It was the first career his Aunt Ramona had suggested that Stephen could stand considering.

"I'll think about applying Aunt Ramona," Stephen said.

"You've only got three more months of school, Stevie," Uncle Marco said, looking up from his laptop. "You know I can get you on. Just say the word."

"What you do is cool, Uncle Marco, but I kinda wanted to look into what Grandpa and Daddy's got brewing in Atlanta."

"You mean murdering people," June said.

"June," Marco warned.

"Murder is killing the innocent," Stephen said. "These people are legally sanctioned to be killed."

"Just because it's legal doesn't make it right," June said.

"Besides, being a Bloodman is a bunch of hurry up and wait," Marco said. "That's why I didn't follow Dad and Antonio into the guild."

"And being a Park Ranger is loaded with adventure?" Stephen said with a smirk.

"Chock full, god dammit," Marco said. "And it's Special Agent, smart ass. Hell, just a week ago, I put away the big boys of this gang of thieves calling themselves the *Archeologists*—they were trafficking in looted artifacts of the Piscataway Conoy Tribe."

Uncle Marco was proud of being an ISB special agent with the National Park Service, which meant that since he moved in with his uncle and aunt when he enrolled in Georgetown University he had heard tales of forest fires and poachers and ruthless gangs called the *Archaeologists* selling Native American treasures on the black market.

"If not a Park Ranger, how about a chef?" Aunt Ramona said. "You like to cook."

"I like to sleep, too," Stephen said. "And you haven't suggested a job as a Sleepologist yet."

"Smart ass," Uncle Marco said, shaking his head.

Stephen snickered.

Aunt Ramona sucked her teeth. She appeared ready to suggest another line of work when the smell of burning metal permeated the room. It was coming from the front door. Or what used to be the door. It had been melted off its hinges.

Uncle Marco saw it too.

"Shit! Get Stephen out of here! Y'all get out now!"

Where the door had been, there stood three men in khaki pants, a khaki safari shirt, brown fedora and brown Chelsea boots. Two of the men were tall, husky— "country strong" Aunt Ramona called it—and one was fat, and of average height.

Ramona took Stephen by the arm but had no chance to escape with him. The fat man already had an *S&W 500* revolver aimed at them.

"Don't move," the man holding the revolver said.

"Dragon Dan," Marco spat. "What's this?"

"You know exactly what this is, Marco. Yeah, we know you're the one behind the mask, who knocked out my little brother's teeth. Playing good cop at the station and shit."

"Dragon Dan, I don't know what you think you—"

Then Marco was dead. The .50 Caliber round had punched a hole the size of a beer bottle cap in his forehead then fragments of bone, gray matter and blood had spattered the wall behind Marco. His body fell out of the cheer and hit the floor with a loud thud.

"Don't move," Dragon Dan shouted.

"Don't even let me see you blink."

Stephen stayed frozen. He could feel his aunt behind him shaking, holding Stephen's arm tightly.

Dragon Dan waved to one of the tall men, who took a small pack from his back. From it he produced a nail gun.

Stephen was keenly aware of every move the men made and aware that his aunt was growing frightened and enraged. It occurred to him as strange that he was not scared, too.

He watched Dragon Dan and the other men take hold of his uncle and prepare to nail him to the doorframe where the door once stood.

Ramona shouted out. Stephen didn't hear what she meant to shout; Dragon Dan was too quick. As soon as a sound passed her lips, he shot her. Stephen felt the hot air pass over his head. He smelled his aunt's blood, but he did not move. It wasn't fear that held Stephen still: he stood knowing that if he moved, he would be shot as well. Stephen heard Ramona's body fall to the floor, then all was silent.

Dragon Dan stared at Stephen.

Stephen stood still and expressionless. He knew Dragon Dan was deciding if he should live or die. The tall men pulled .40 Caliber *G-22 Glock* pistols from their waists then waited for the order.

Stephen gave the gangsters nothing to inspire his demise.

Dragon Dan quietly turned his back, leaving the gunmen to keep an eye on Stephen as he knelt down to Marco's body.

One of the tall men came to Dragon Dan's side and helped him with the corpse. They tried to prop him up to the wall, but Dragon Dan was too short, and he let the arm slip. Marco's corpse fell halfway to the floor. The other tall man turned to see if they needed help. For a fraction of a second, he took his eyes from Stephen and let his pistol drift a few centimeters off target. In that instant, Stephen showed an extraordinary skill he never knew he had.

Through the entire episode he had remained oddly, totally detached. The emotional impact of his family's death didn't register so much as the acute awareness of how it had happened. Stephen saw how they were struggling with his uncle's body. He knew that behind him, his aunt had fallen in a position that could trip one of the men if he was not careful. He knew with utter clarity that for the moment all three men had their eyes off him.

Stephen knew as soon as the man's eyes were turned that they might not turn again. He knew that if he was shot by the small nail gun, at this distance it wouldn't be fatal, not immediately. He knew that there was no way they could let him live after this, and only briefly did he wonder why Dragon Dan hadn't ordered his death a second ago. It only took him another instant to decide what to do.

The gunman was standing within a yard of him, his finger off the trigger. His grip looked loose.

Stephen put that to the test and

grabbed the pistol. He was wrong; the tall man's grip was quite firm.

Now that the tall man knew what Stephen was doing, his element of surprise was at an end. He thought it best to surprise him further by twisting the weapon away from himself and toward the other tall man with the nail gun. That proved a good idea when the gun went off and a bullet hit the man with the nail gun just to the left of the bridge of his nose, knocking his eye out of the socket and onto the floor as splinters of bone and a fine mist of blood flew into the air.

Stephen saw that Dragon Dan was slow in recognizing the threat. The gangster was putting all he had into wresting the pistol away from Stephen, so he kicked downward onto the gangster shin, the heel of Stephen's shoe cracking off a piece of the gangster's shin. As he expected, the tall man screamed in agony, but he did not let go of the pistol.

Stephen kicked the man in the other shin.

The gangster still didn't let go of the pistol, but he did fall to his knees.

Stephen kicked again, driving the instep of his foot up into the gangster's groin.

That loosened his grip.

Stephen pulled the weapon from the gangster and moved it to his other hand, letting go of the barrel and gripping the handle firmly, finger on the trigger. He pulled the trigger.

The gangster fell onto his back, blood leaking from a hole in the back of his head.

Knowing he had a better idea of the house's layout than Gangster Dan, Stephen ran through the kitchen and around the corner, down a hall and into the bathroom. Then he hid behind the door.

Dragon Dan pushed the door open.

Stephen slammed it on his hand.

Dragon Dan screamed and dropped the revolver. He didn't bother to pick it up; instead, he rammed his shoulder into the door and barged in hard and fast.

He burst in with such strength Stephen had no problem pushing Dragon Dan farther, forcing his head down into the toilet. Stephen then lay his chest on the back of Dragon's Dan's head and bore down with his weight and strength.

Dragon Dan struggled to free his face from the toilet water. His arms flailed wildly for several long seconds and then fell limp.

Stephen remained lying on Dragon Dan for another minute to be sure the gangster was dead. He left the bathroom with great caution, looking around for anyone else who might have entered. He found the two tall gangsters on the dining room floor, unmoving.

After glancing outside the melted door, he was satisfied that the immediate danger was over. He ran out of the house and into the cool evening night.

"I'm coming home," Stephen whispered.

He was going to be a Bloodman after all.

THE MAILMAN

The little girl was supposed to be with the others. She should have been hiding in the *school*, huddled next to other students in the cafeteria as a precaution against stray bullets. She was *not* supposed to be directly in the path of an advancing gang of killers.

The Mailman cursed. He patched his smart glasses into the Bloodmen's observation drone, which circled three thousand feet above. A quick rewind of the video footage showed exactly what had happened.

He followed the figure of the girl as she peeled off, unseen, from the group of other children being shepherded to safety by an old woman. He saw as the skinny child duck into a doorway, waiting while a pair of *Bratva* rushed past, and then dart after them down the narrow streets. He cursed again when he saw the girl slip right past the line of defenses on the edge of Maputo, and climb to a vantage point along the rocky hills by the side of the road.

The footage showed the outcrop below the girl give way, causing her to lose her footing and tumble down the hill in a cloud of dust. The Mailman switched back to a real-time view, where he saw the girl lying on the ground, her leg pinned under a rock, her frail body right beside the road that, even now, Sergei Mogilevich's 'Prizraki Smerti'—*Death Ghosts*—were advancing along.

The Bratva were pushing to become a Guild and knew that if they delivered Mozambique to Russia, they'd be sanctioned. The Bloodmen had been paid a lot of money to make sure that didn't happen.

The miniature rock slide had thrown dust and gravel into the air, there was no way the *Bratva*, watching the road intently, could have missed it. Still, the Mailman hoped.

"Kamara," the Mailman said in a low voice. The small bud in his ear picked it up. "We've got a kid on the board; a little girl. You see her?"

Nearly nine thousand miles away, in the Ile of the Bloodmen, newly appointed Guild Professor Kamara Keita replied, "Yes." His rich baritone voice betrayed a nervous excitement.

Another window opened up in the Mailman's smart glasses. On the screen was Berkeley, who had been recruited into the Bloodmen out of Special Forces right along with the Mailman. "Bruh, we've got a problem," Berkeley said.

"Yeah I see her, we're going to—"

"Not the little girl," Berkeley said. "Look at grid J13."

The Mailman switched the view in his smart glasses again, until he was looking down on the line of built-up defenses he had helped reinforce on the edge of town. From one of the fortified houses, fattened by sandbags and bristling with machine gun barrels, he saw four soldiers creeping past the foxholes and barbed wire, toward the road and the supine figure of the girl.

"God dammit," the Mailman hissed, switching to the radio channel he and Ungulani Gungunhana, the commander of Mozambique's Special Forces Group 2, had agreed upon. "Ungulani, where are your men going?"

The reply, curt and scratchy, came immediately, "To get Ayane."

The Mailman rolled his eyes. "Negative, Ungulani," the Mailman said, "Hold location. "We'll ensure the Death Ghosts never reaches her."

Ayane Gungunhana was Ungulani's granddaughter, and the commander doted on the girl immensely. He had even let her sit in on the planning meetings, as Gungunhana and Kamara went over fields of fire, approach probabilities, and fallback positions. The young girl had looked on in unconcealed awe, as much for her grandfather as for the mountain of a man, Kamara, towering over everyone else in the room.

The Mailman's map overlay in his smart glasses showed the five red icons of Berkeley's team of Bloodmen along the hills on the western side of town, overlooking the road.

His own team was opposite Berkeley's, concealed behind scrub brush and within shallow, hastily dug foxholes. Gungunhana's hardened *soldiers* lined the defenses along the edge of town. The Mailman was on his belly in the dirt, settled in next to Lou Dean, a former

CIA Black Ops operative who had been recruited into the Bloodmen after being fired from the 'Company' for exposing its racism.

The Mozambican commander didn't reply, and he and his men continued moving through the defenses toward the road.

"Damn," the Mailman said, shaking his head. "Berkeley, see if you can talk some sense into Gungunhana, I'll try to buy more time."

"O dara."

The overhead view in the Mailman's glasses showed the plume of dust where Mogilevich's Prizraki Smerti was advancing along the road, capturing hundreds of Mozambican soldiers.

The Mailman spoke again into his radio, "Kamara?"

"I've got full control of the drone," Kamara said. "No tracking by the Bratva."

"Good. Drop it and patch me into its speakers."

"O dara," the young Guild Professor said.

The Mailman brought up the window showing the camera feed from the drone and watched as it angled tightly toward the line of Bratva below, guided expertly by Kamara.

It was close enough now for the Mailman to pick out olive drab jumpsuit-clad figures, faces covered with black balaclavas, Vityaz-SN submachine guns glinting. Several heads turned upward.

He engaged the speakers and said in Russian, "Attention: you are entering territory legally protected by The Bloodmen. Turn back now or be fired upon."

He was about to repeat the message when a dozen flashes flared up simultaneously from the ground, and the picture from the drone skewed violently before cutting out to black.

Mogilevich's Ghosts of Death spread out, keeping space between each Bratva special operative, and then surged forward until they were close enough to see Gungunhana and the other three *Mozambican soldiers*, still running to Ayane's prostrate form. The Mailman saw puffs of dust kick up around the feet of the sprinting Mozambicans as bullets whipped toward them. One man staggered, hit in the shoulder, but lowered his head again and kept running.

As the Mailman watched, Gungunhana and his men reached the pinned girl, diving into cover behind a large rock. It was scant protection from the submachine guns and pistol fire now concentrated on their little force.

"Berkeley," the Mailman called into his radio, "Lay down covering fire for Ungulani and his men. Concentrate on anyone getting too close."

"O dara," Berkeley said.

The five Mozambican soldiers opened up with a hail of bullets from their FN FAL rifles, 7.62mm rounds felling a dozen Bratva.

With his glasses the Mailman zoomed onto Gungunhana's gruff face as he crouched behind the rock, which was barely big enough to protect him or his granddaughter, let alone

his other three men. Two of them were pushing, leaning their shoulders into the stone, the
girl was screaming. One of the soldiers, lying
prone and firing his rifle at nearby targets,
suddenly jerked and slumped forward, his
body still.

"Damn," the Mailman sighed.

"Lou," the Mailman said, turning to the
man on his left.
Lou nodded. "O dara," he said.
Lou signaled the other Bloodmen.
The Mailman lifted himself into a crouch
and raised his Barrett MRAD Mk23 precision
rifle.
"Suppressive fire!" Lou yelled.
The roar of rifles from the Bloodmen
under Lou's order thundered across the sky
and the Mailman sprang up, charging down
the hill, his focus on the four soldiers huddled
behind the rock on the side of the road.
Before he was even halfway there, he
heard the distinctive crack of bullets being
fired in his direction. One whistled past his
head, another slammed into the packed dirt of
the roadway in front of him. He ran faster,
forcing his legs to push harder. As he reached
the rock he slid onto his side into the scant
cover beside the other men.
Gungunhana's wide eyes showed he
hadn't expected the Mailman to risk his life
like this.
The Mailman grabbed the commander's
shoulder and shouted to be heard over the

racket of bullets hitting stone, "Where do I push?"

The militia commander pointed, and the Mailman joined with him and one of the surviving soldiers as they heaved against the stubborn rock. The Mailman's feet dug into the dirt. Gungunhana grunted. Finally, it moved, lifting slightly into the air. The third *soldier* pulled the little girl back, sliding her out from underneath the rock. She screamed again. As soon as she was clear the Mailman and the soldiers let go and the rock crashed down.

"We need to get out of here!" the Mailman shouted. "Get her arms, I'll cover!"

Gungunhana and another soldier scooped up the girl between them as the Mailman turned back to the advancing enemy. He brought the rifle's scope to his eye and squeezed off a round at a group of men coming up the other side of the road. A Bratva operative's head snapped back, sending a mist of blood into the sky behind him. He fell. The Mailman charged the bolt and fired again, dropping another Bratva. The another. The remaining Bratva fell back.

He risked a glance behind him in time to see one of the *Mozambican soldiers* take a round to his neck. He crumpled, losing his grip on the injured girl and pulling Gungunhana down with the sudden unbalanced weight.

Without thinking, the Mailman stood, firing the last round off blindly behind him as he ran to Gungunhana and the last surviving soldier. He swung the rifle to his back and kept running.

He was almost there when a round hit him in the leg, sending him tumbling forward into the hard dirt. A sudden blooming of pain told him the bullet had broken his lower shin. He struggled to his feet and limped the last few yards to the pair of soldiers.

The Mailman was helping Gungunhana to stand when another slug hit him in the back, shoving him forward. The Mailman went down again, dozens of bullets chewing up the road around him. Gungunhana was yelling something but the noise of the enemy rifles, and the pain in the Bloodman's leg and back, made it impossible for the Mailman to hear him.

But he heard something else. Something on the edge of his perception. Something familiar.

The Mailman stopped, looking around as he listened. Then he saw them, two dozen Bloodmen—the best assassins in the world—descending upon the Bratva.

Bodies disappeared in a cloud of dust and blood. Men in olive drab jumpsuits screamed, threw down their rifles and ran, or ducked into even the faintest of hollows in the ground for cover, hoping to be spared.

In his glasses, the Mailman could see the Bratva beating a hasty retreat. It was over.

* * *

Ayane lay in a hospital bed, her leg

straight out in front of her, set in a cast.

She looked up from her bed at the Mailman as he approached.

The Mailman smiled, but the little girl didn't return the expression.

Instead she stared at him, her eyes wide. "It has only been three days," she said. "How are you already up walking while I'm still in this cast and you were more injured than me?"

"We Bloodmen have a mushroom from the Zulu that helps us block out pain," the Mailman said. "I'm still healing, though."

"I need some of those—how do your people say... 'shrooms?"

The Mailman laughed. "Not those kinds of mushrooms."

"So, you'll be leaving soon?"

The mailman shook his head. "Mogilevich's army hasn't been broken, just beaten. They'll be back. And the Bloodmen always complete a contract."

Balogun Ojetade

As a former combat veteran (MOS: 18F), Master and Technical Director of the Afrikan Martial Arts Institute and Co-Chair of the Urban Survival and Preparedness Institute, Balogun Ojetade is the author of the bestselling non-fiction books *Afrikan Martial Arts: Discovering the Warrior Within, The Afrikan Warriors Bible, Surviving the Urban Apocalypse, The Urban Self Defense Manual, The Young Afrikan Warriors' Guide to Defeating Bullies & Trolls, Never Unarmed: The Afrikan Warriors' Guide to Improvised Weapons, Ofo Ase: 365 Daily Affirmations to Awaken the Afrikan Warrior Within, Ori: The Afrikan Warriors' Mindset, Ogun Ye! Protecting the Afrikan Family and Community, Kori O: Protecting Afrikan Children from Violence & Sexual Abuse,* and *SKG: The Black Man & Woman's Guide to Sticks, Knives and Guns.*

He is one of the leading authorities on Afrofuturism and Afroretroism—film, fashion or fiction that combines African and/or African American culture with a blend of "retro" styles and futuristic technology, in order to explore the themes of tension between past and future and between the alienating and empowering effects of technology and on Creative Resistance. He writes about Afrofuturism/Afroretroism—Sword & Soul, Rococoa, Steamfunk and Dieselfunk at http://chroniclesofharriet.com/.

He is author of twenty-five novels and game-books – *MOSES: The Chronicles of Harriet Tubman (Books 1 & 2); The Chronicles of Harriet Tubman: Freedonia; Redeemer; Once Upon*

A Time In Afrika; Fist of Africa; A Single Link; Wrath of the Siafu; The Scythe; The Keys; Redeemer: The Cross Chronicles; Beneath the Shining Jewel; Q-T-Pies: The Savannah Swan Files (Book 0) and *A Haunting in the SWATS: The Savannah Swan Files (Book 1); Siafu Saves the World; Siafu vs. The Horde; Dembo's Ditty; The Beatdown; Initiate 16; Gunsmoke Blues; Malik: Confessions of a Black Identity Extremist; Malik: Confessions of a Black Identity Extremist 2: Enemy of the State; Granma's Hand; Kill City* and *Steamfunkateers: The Steamfunk Role Playing Game* and the Steamfunkateers adventure, *The Haunting of the House of Crum*—contributing co-editor of three anthologies: *Ki: Khanga: The Anthology, Steamfunk* and *Dieselfunk* and contributing editor of the *Rococoa* anthology and *Black Power: The Superhero Anthology.*

He is also the creator and author of the Afrofuturistic manga series, *Jagunjagun Lewa (Pretty Warrior)*, author/co-creator of the *Ice-Cold Carter* photo-graphic novel series and co-author of the *Ngolo* comic book series.

Finally, he is co-author of the award-winning screenplay, *Ngolo* and co-creator of *Ki Khanga: The Sword and Soul Role-Playing Game,* both with author Milton Davis.

Reach him on Facebook at https://www.facebook.com/Afrikan.Martial.Ar ts and on Instagram at @balogun_ojetade and @afrikanmartialarts.

Milton Davis

Milton Davis is an award winning Black Speculative fiction writer and owner of MVmedia, LLC, a small publishing company specializing in Science Fiction, Fantasy and Sword and Soul. MVmedia's mission is to provide speculative fiction books that represent people of color in a positive manner. Milton is the author of nineteen novels; his most recent is the post-apocalyptic adventure

Gunman's Peace. He is the editor and co-editor of seven anthologies; *The City, Dark Universe* with Gene Peterson; *Griots: A Sword and Soul Anthology and Griot: Sisters of the Spear,* with Charles R. Saunders; *The Ki Khanga Anthology,* the *Steamfunk! Anthology,* and the *Dieselfunk anthology* with Balogun Ojetade. Milton's work had also been featured in *Black Power: The Superhero Anthology and Rococoa published by Roaring Lions Productions; Skelos 2: The Journal of Weird Fiction and Dark Fantasy Volume 2, Steampunk Writers Around the World* published by Luna Press; *Heroika: Dragoneaters* published by First Perseid Press, and *Bass Reeves Frontier Marshal Volume Two.* Milton Davis and Balogun Ojetade won the 2014 Urban Action Showcase Award for Best Script; Milton's story 'The Swarm' was nominated for the 2018 British Science Fiction Association Award for Short Fiction.

Be sure to check out Ngolo Diaspora #1
www.mvmediaatl.com

OJETADE/DAVIS

Ngolo Diaspora #2

Coming 2021!